"Trace Conger is establishing himself as one of the most original voices in crime fiction." - Gregory Petersen, author of *Open Mike* and *The Dream Thief*

"Mirage Man is a propulsive novel that churns with energy and tension." - Vick Mickunas, NPR's Book Nook

"Conger's writing is direct. It moves clearly and quickly, perfect for thrillers." - Ronald Tierney, author of the Deets Shanahan Mysteries

"The Mr. Finn series breathes new life into the P.I. genre... It is one of the best detective series I've ever read." - Gumshoes, Gats and Gams

"*The Prison Guard's Son* is a superbly crafted crime novel. The characters are richly drawn with a rare combination of nuance and depth... This is one of the year's best books." - Mysterious Reviews

"*The Shadow Broker* tips a handsome hat in the direction of old-fashioned pulp fiction and it does so with considerable style. The writing is fluid and the plot pumps along." - Murder, Mayhem & More

TRACE CONGER

CATCH AND RELEASE

A CONNOR HARDING THRILLER

Catch and Release

Copyright © 2022 by Trace Conger

Cover design by 100Covers.

Interior design and formatting by the handsome devils at

Black Mill Books

ISBN-13: 978-1-957336-02-2

Printed in the United States of America

Library of Congress Cataloging-in-Publication Data

Conger, Trace

Catch and Release (A Connor Harding Novel) — 1st edition

For Beth.

Inspiration can be hard to find. You make it easy.

Thank you for filling my life with joy, love, and optimism.

1

THE MAN IN THE CANOE

CONNOR HARDING WATCHED from the front porch as the man with the shoebox in his lap paddled the rented canoe toward the dock. He was a few hundred feet out, and the wind wasn't cooperating. That, combined with the angry lake, tossed the canoe from side to side, almost upending it.

The middle-aged man inside the boat was imposing. He probably played football in his younger days. His solid frame, an asset in most situations, worked against him in the small canoe, which rocked back and forth, fighting the wind.

The lake toyed with him. Every time he aligned the front of the canoe with the dock, a gust knocked him off course and spun him in the choppy water.

Setting his binoculars down, Connor left the porch and walked to the dock. Generations of soft moss and decaying pine needles soothed the bottoms of his bare feet. When he reached the water, he noticed the man in the canoe wasn't any closer.

He sat on the edge of the dock, plunged his feet in the cool water, and refocused his gaze on the man struggling against the wind. For a moment, he considered firing up the pontoon boat tied to the other side of the boathouse, going out, and towing the canoe in. But that would mean a trip back to the main house for the boat key, a lot of work for a man on vacation.

Another five minutes, and the canoe was close enough. Connor stood up, grabbed a nearby rope, and tossed it out, keeping a firm grip on one end. It landed across the big man's shoulder. The oar slipped from his hand when he reached for the rope, but somehow he managed to secure both without capsizing. After he wedged the shoebox between his thighs, he laid the oar across the canoe and looked for a place to tie off the rope.

"Just hold on to it," yelled Connor. "I'll pull you in."

The man complied, and a few moments later, Connor had pulled him to the dock.

"Tie your line to the cleat and watch your step getting out. Those things tip real easy."

The man released his vice-like grip on the shoebox, placed it on the dock, and used the oar to push it as far from the edge as possible. Then he took the bowline and looked up at Connor.

"What's a cleat?"

"That metal thing on the edge of the dock." Connor kicked it for emphasis.

"Right." The man wrapped the line around the cleat and tied it off with a knot Connor had never seen.

"First time in Maine?" said Connor.

"Yes." The man clumsily climbed out of the canoe and retrieved the shoebox.

As he stood up, Connor took him all in. He was even bigger than expected. Six-foot-four, at least. The man was in his late thirties. He had wind-blown hair that Connor assumed had been neatly combed before he climbed into Mitch Skinner's canoe. The expensive slacks and dress shoes said he'd either never spent time on a lake before or didn't have time to pack a proper bag. He looked important. Too important to take a commercial flight into Bangor and drive the two-plus hours to Meddybemps Lake. No, he had likely chartered a private plane into Eastport Municipal Airport, twenty-five miles away.

"Boone," said the man.

Connor waved him toward the house. "I was starting to think you weren't coming. Mitch radioed me when you left the town dock an hour ago."

"I had a hard time on the lake. The wind kept pushing me around."

"Yeah, it'll do that. Why didn't Mitch give you the motorboat? You could have made the trip in ten minutes."

"He said there wasn't a motorboat."

Connor sneered. "There's a motorboat. He's just screwing with you."

The wind picked up and the shoebox lid lifted from the box, but the big man snapped it back down.

"Let's get this over with," said Connor, leading the way up the worn path to the main house.

When they reached the porch, Connor opened a second folding chair and placed it across from the one he'd been sitting in earlier. "Have a seat."

"I appreciate you meeting with me," said Boone. "My employer does too."

"I normally don't talk business on vacation, but I'm hearing you out as a favor to my brother."

Boone nodded and opened the shoebox. "How much has your brother told you?"

"He said someone murdered your boss's wife and kid, what, ten years ago?"

"Twelve," he corrected. "Debra and Sydney."

"Right. And now he wants to find whoever's responsible."

"That's the bones of it."

"He also said your employer, Little Freddie, is it?"

"That's right."

"Said he's wrapped up with some pretty bad people. Seems obvious the murders and his job are connected." Connor nodded to the shoebox. "That the evidence?"

"Yes." Boone opened the box and handed it to Connor.

Inside were a dozen postcards.

"He gets one every year on the anniversary of the murders," said Boone. "Taunting him."

Connor plucked them out and flipped through them. Some had photos of famous landmarks, like the Hoover Dam and Yellowstone. Others were black and white photos of people playing instruments or dancing. Some were reproductions of famous paintings. But it wasn't the photos Connor was interested in. It was the writing on the back. Connor held one up, tilting it just right to catch the narrow sunbeam coming in from between the pine trees.

Sydney screamed. Your wife didn't. I think she was trying to keep a brave face for her daughter. I bet she thought if she wasn't afraid, your daughter wouldn't be afraid either. I guess it doesn't matter much, but I killed your wife first.

He tossed it back into the shoebox and picked up another.

Tiptoes wore a dancer's outfit the night I stabbed her. Some shiny red thing with fringe. It was the same color as her blood. I kept her dance shoes.

"And he gets one every year?" asked Connor.

"Like clockwork."

"Is there anything in here that gives us a lead on who's sending them?"

"No. Just taunts. Details about the murders, but nothing about the killer or anything else that sheds light on who's behind it."

"You're sure?"

"Freddie's read those a million times. He'd have noticed an important detail if it was in there."

Connor noted the postmark on the card. San Diego. "It's obviously connected to someone your boss had a run-in with. Why not cross-reference a list of Freddie's enemies with anyone he knows in San Diego?"

"Look at the other postmarks."

Connor flipped to another card. Cody, Wyoming. He

looked at another. New York, New York. And another. Lincoln, Ohio.

"They're from all over," said Boone. "No two were sent from the same city. And Freddie isn't convinced the murders were connected to his job."

"Bullshit. He's a contract killer. It's connected."

"No one knew that when this happened. His own family didn't know. His wife thought he was a business consultant."

"Someone knew."

"Then that's who you need to find."

"Why me?"

"Because your brother owes Little Freddie a favor. And we hear you're good at finding people." Boone stood up. "So we expect you to get started." He reached into his sock, removed a cell phone, and handed it to Connor. "There's a number in the contact list. Freddie will be waiting for updates."

"You always keep a phone in your sock?"

"You saw the size of that canoe. Where was I supposed to put it?"

Connor took the phone and tossed it into the shoebox with the postcards. "That's not going to work on the island. Only the mainland." He snatched a boat key from the decaying table next to the front door. "Follow me."

He led Boone down to the boathouse and around the dock to the pontoon boat. He fired the two MerCruiser engines, untied the lines, and eased away from the dock. When he was far enough out, he threw the throttle down and put 400-horsepower behind them. They were at the town dock in minutes. Connor didn't bother tying up. He wasn't going to be there long.

After Boone stepped onto the dock, he wrapped his thick hands around the boat's aluminum frame and leaned back in.

"We expect results, Connor. Freddie isn't someone you want to owe favors."

"I don't owe him anything."

"No, you don't. But your brother does."

As Boone walked toward the black Mercedes in the small parking lot, Connor threw the throttle down and tore away from the dock. Once he made it to the middle of the lake, he killed the engine and clicked on the marine radio. He popped the receiver off the unit and pressed the button with his thumb.

"Mitch, you there?"

He waited for a bit and then tried again.

"Mitch here, over."

"This is Connor. You can pick up your busted-ass canoe at my dock."

"What happened to your visitor?"

"Just dropped him off. Figured that was faster than sending him back in your rental. Why didn't you give him the motorboat?"

"Because I pegged him as an asshole," said Mitch. "Was he?"

"Too soon to tell."

Connor was about to throw the throttle again when Mitch squawked back on the radio.

"Not sure if it's worth mentioning, but there was another fella in the car with the big guy."

"That right?"

"Yeah. He got out of the car and went into the community center. Probably for the AC. Older fella. Short white hair. Wore a black turtleneck and gray slacks. Obviously not from around here."

"Thanks for the info," said Connor. "I suspect I'll run into him sooner or later."

He clicked off the radio, buried the throttle, and returned to the cabin to get his fishing gear.

2

NOT MY PIG

CONNOR HAD COME to his family's cabin on Meddybemps Lake to fish. The place was remote, and besides fishing, the only thing there was to do out there was nothing, which Connor also liked. After two hours of fighting smallmouth bass in his favorite cove, Connor hauled up the boat anchor and headed for the town dock. Every summer, the Harding family rented dock space from Mitch Skinner across the lake, and Conner would usually tie up there whenever he went to the mainland. That wasn't the destination today. Connor was headed to Palmer's Restaurant and Grocery for a late lunch, and the town dock was much closer to the restaurant than Mitch's place.

Except for the two fishing boats Connor passed, the lake was deserted. Meddybemps Lake didn't like boaters. It was full of rocks the size of Volkswagens that turned steel boat props into confetti. The lake froze to three feet every winter, and the melting ice moved even the giant rocks, so those boat crushers were not in the same place year after year. The only ones who trusted a boat on Meddybemps Lake were townies who had lived there long enough to know the areas to avoid. Connor wasn't a townie, but his family had owned the cabin for close to a hundred years, and he'd been coming here since he could walk. The only thing that betrayed him as an outsider was his lack of a Down East accent.

Connor eased up to the town dock, tied off the lines, killed the engine, and stepped off the pontoon boat onto the weathered cedar planks. On one side of the dock were a boat launch and a small parking lot. On the other side was the Meddybemps Community Center, which served as a town meeting hall, event center, and post office. It was usually empty. Connor passed the building and walked the quarter-mile path along the lake edge until he arrived at Palmer's.

Palmer's Restaurant and Grocery was just that, part restaurant and part grocery. There were about 150 residents in Meddybemps and not much else. Aside from the chain grocery store in Calais, Maine, which was a good forty minutes away, Palmer's was the only place to pick up ice, milk, bait, propane, and beer. It was also the place to find townies trading news and tales of fishing, logging, and anything else.

Connor stepped inside and found Jack Palmer, the owner, cook, bartender, waiter, and grocery clerk, reading a three-day-old newspaper.

"Jack."

"Connor." Jack looked up from his paper. "You shop'n or eat'n?"

"Came in for some clams, if you've got any left."

Jack tossed the paper on the counter and walked into the restaurant side of the building. "Think I can scrounge something up fer ya."

Connor followed Jack into the restaurant and went for his favorite booth, near the back next to the pool table.

A few minutes later, an older man wearing a black turtleneck and gray slacks walked in. His short white hair reflected the glare from the ceiling lights. When they locked eyes, the man approached and stood over Connor.

"You know I'm on vacation, right?" said Connor. "I come to Maine to get away from people."

"I thought it was important we talk."

Connor didn't have to ask who the man was. He already knew. Little Freddie was a killer who worked for various Midwest crime families. He'd never met him, but his brother, Finn, had worked with him years ago, and he'd given Connor all the juicy details. The rumor was that Freddie had been a high school history teacher back in the day. At some point, he discovered a knack for killing people and changed careers. He was in high demand because he enjoyed his job. Killing is a gruesome business, and most of those who do it for a living don't quite care for it. Freddie was different. He liked it. He looked forward to it the same way a nurse looks forward to delivering a newborn. That's some crazy shit, but say what you want about Little Freddie, he was in the right line of work.

Little Freddie sat down without asking. "I can't stress how important it is that you find the person sending those postcards."

"You haven't given me much to go on, but as I told your friend, it seems the murders were retaliation for something you did. I figure you already know who was behind it."

"I've done a lot of bad things. Hurt more people than I can count. It could be anyone."

Connor thought for a moment. "Why now?"

"What?"

"This happened twelve years ago. Why only start looking into this now?"

Little Freddie looked down at the table and then up at Connor. "I guess I thought there wasn't enough evidence to go on. Now, I have twelve cards, twelve pieces of evidence. Hopefully, there's enough there to help you."

"Why not make things easier for me? Give me a list of the best candidates. You've got to have an idea. I need something to start with."

"I can't do that."

"Look, here's how this works. I'm going to help you as a favor to my brother, who obviously owes you something. I'll look into it while I'm on vacation, but then I go back to my life. That means you only have a sliver of my time. Give me something to work with, and I can use that time to your advantage. Hold vital information from me, and I'll spend that time spinning my wheels and you won't get much."

"I'm not holding information back. I honestly don't know who it could be."

Jack walked into the room and placed a glass of ice water and a basket of fried clams on the table.

Connor inhaled, taking in the scent of cayenne pepper. "Thanks, Jack. Looks perfect."

Jack looked at Little Freddie. "Getcha a menu?"

"No," said Connor. "He's not staying."

Little Freddie waited for Jack to leave before speaking again.

"Your brother said you were good with things like this."

"I am good with things like this. But I'm no magician. If there's nothing there, there's nothing there."

"There's something there, and you better find it." Little Freddie stood up. "You don't want to owe me."

"I don't owe you shit."

"Your brother does."

"Not my pig, not my farm."

Little Freddie leaned against the table and came in close. "Come up empty, and you and your brother are going to have a problem."

"I don't know too much about you." Connor popped a clam in his mouth. "But I do know one thing."

"What's that?"

"I know you're not the most dangerous person in this room."

"I hope we won't have to find out." He turned and walked toward the door. "I'll be in touch."

"Can't wait," said Connor, taking a napkin from the metal dispenser on the table.

3

POSTCARD ANATOMY

AFTER POLISHING off his last clam, Connor crinkled the stiff paper liner into a ball and set it inside the red plastic basket. Then he downed the glass of water. The ice cubes hit the back of his throat, almost gagging him. He sat for a moment, savoring the meal he had just finished and taking in the quietness of the restaurant. Everything was still, like the rest of the world ended at the restaurant door, and he was the only thing that existed. Maine was always calm. Besides the monster smallmouth bass gliding through the lake, that stillness was the reason he escaped here. But he knew this trip was now different. That calm was fleeting.

Connor left a twenty on the table and ducked out the side door. He walked back along the worn path toward the town dock contemplating how to find the person on the other end of the postcards. He had almost reached the dock when he stopped and turned back around.

The Meddybemps Community Center needed a paint job. The summer sun had done a number on the cedar planks, and no one seemed eager to do anything about it. In addition to hosting monthly meetings for the Meddybemps Lake Conservation Society, random Bingo Nights, and the local firefighters' fundraiser, the building also housed the Meddybemps Post Office.

Until a few years ago, the post office was in Dorris Miller's kitchen. When she died, whoever decided such things moved the post office into the community center. It was still a small operation. There was a mail sorting room, which was the size of a commercial walk-in freezer, a small office with a single desk, and a front counter where a clerk sold stamps and collected parcels.

Some two dozen island homes dotted the lake, and since the US Postal Service hadn't yet invested in a fleet of boats to deliver mail to those properties, the residents each had a mail slot behind the front counter.

The brunette with long wavy hair, permanent smile, and light blue shirt with a USPS logo was Dana Walton. She was one of two postal workers who split their time between working in the office and delivering mail in the wood-paneled station wagon parked out front.

"Hey, Connor."

"Dana."

She scanned the mailboxes behind the counter and turned with disappointed eyes. "Sorry, no mail for you. Expecting something?"

"Nope. Got a question for you, though."

"Shoot."

"You know any postal inspectors?"

"I dated one in Bangor a few years back. I think he's dead now."

"Well, that won't help."

"Why do you ask?"

"I'm helping someone out." Connor leaned against the counter like he belonged there. "He's receiving anonymous postcards in the mail."

"What kind of postcards? Are they threatening or harassing? If so, he can file a claim with his local post office and they can investigate it."

"He's not the type of person to go to the authorities. More of a do-it-yourself kind of guy."

"And he wants to figure out who's sending them?"

"Right."

"Well, that's going to be tough. No name or anything?"

"Nope. That's why I want to talk to a postal inspector. To see how they'd go about investigating it. Maybe there's something printed on a postcard they could track. Like that barcode on the bottom?"

Dana thought for a moment, then turned to the mail slots, grabbed something, and turned back.

"So, here's a postcard Pete Jenkins got." She flipped it over and pointed to a narrow white label that ran horizontally across the bottom of the card. Short black hash marks ran the length of the strip. "You see this? The post office in the origin city adds this. It's coded information that includes a three-digit mail sectional center."

"Is that for where the postcard is processed or where it's going?"

"Destination only. It's an internal code to help us route the card through the appropriate facilities to get to this particular mailbox. If you're looking for processing info, the only thing that will help is the postage cancellation stamp." She pointed to the black ink mark over the stamp with Old

Glory. "They cancel the postage with a rubber stamp. It's got the date and the office location where the postcard was mailed. So, at least your friend can determine the city the postcards came from."

"So, that's it then, no secret postal-service-only information hidden on there anywhere?"

"Afraid not. No secret watermarks or address data. We're the post office, not the CIA."

"That's what I was afraid of."

"Your friend should really contact the postal service. They have a harassment hotline. It's on the website. Not sure how they would investigate it, but at least they could open a formal investigation."

"Thanks, Dana."

"You bet."

Connor slipped through the front door and headed to his boat, the taste of fried clams still lingering in his throat.

4

MURDERS, MAPS, AND MOTIVES

BACK AT THE ISLAND, Connor rummaged through the upstairs bedroom, a room the family had designated as an official storage room for items too burdensome to throw away. On one wall, a box spring mattress leaned next to an outboard boat motor from the fifties. A handful of fishing poles stood watch in the corner next to an old storage trunk that Connor believed came with the cabin. Along another wall, a green plastic slide, a remnant of Connor's youth, waited quietly to topple over and slice open some unsuspecting ankle.

Connor ignored those items, instead focusing on the warped pine dresser in the corner. It was in there, somewhere. He was wrist-deep in the third drawer when he found it; a folded map of the United States. It was under a navy blue sweatshirt with a sea captain on the front. He took the map, careful not to tear its thin, yellowing edges, and went downstairs, minding the narrow steps. He tacked the map to the wall in the sunroom, then retrieved Freddie's shoebox of postcards and a pink highlighter from the junk drawer and went to work.

After a few minutes of effort, Connor stepped back and stared at the map, zeroing in on the pink circles around a dozen cities: Tampa, Florida; Lincoln, Ohio; San Diego, California; Cody, Wyoming; New York, New York; Flower Mound, Texas; Jefferson City, Missouri; Estes Park, Colorado; Devil's Lake, North Dakota; Catasauqua, Pennsylvania; West Yellowstone, Montana; and Duluth, Minnesota.

The sender had gone to a lot of trouble to collect a seemingly random hoard of postmarks, but were they random? Did the sender travel the country himself, dropping the cards in each of these cities, or did he mail them to an associate in those areas who sent them on his behalf to create the illusion the sender was nomadic?

Connor's brother told him that Little Freddie lived north of Cincinnati and was as murky as they come. He was a cleanup man, the person you call when you've made a mess or needed to make one. From what Connor understood, he worked as a freelancer for any criminal who could afford him. He wasn't loyal to one particular organization.

That business model was good for Little Freddie's bank account but bad for his health. Anyone not loyal to an organization is a risk. Maybe that was why his wife and daughter ended up dead. It was a message to Little Freddie to keep his mouth shut or not fuck with them. Or, maybe he had already fucked with them, and the murders were the recourse.

It was likely Little Freddie's business took him all over the country, but Lincoln, Ohio, was suspicious because it was so close to Freddie's home turf. Connor's theory was that the killer lived in one of the areas the postcards had been sent from, but used the others to obscure his location. Lincoln was too damn close to be random.

Connor shuffled the postcards in his hands and inspected the handwritten messages. He was no handwriting expert, but the straight letters and hard angles suggested the writer was a male. The handwriting also looked consistent on all the cards, which meant one person had churned them out.

He read on. The messages either taunted Little Freddie or provided intimate details about the killings. They described what his wife and daughter were wearing, what they said, or how they acted before he snuffed the life out of them. For all the ghoulish details the notes provided, they offered no specifics on who committed the murders or why.

He turned the cards over and studied the images on the backs. Some included familiar landmarks, while others were more obscure. One was simply a covered bridge that could have been from any small American town. The postcard from Cody, Wyoming, had a black-and-white photograph of Buffalo Bill Cody. The card from Estes Park, Colorado, had an image of an ornate white building, perhaps a hotel or resort, but there was no caption to identify the photo.

All of the postcards were worn, giving the impression they were much older than they should be. Even the one sent this year, the most recent postcard, looked decades old. Perhaps the sender purchased all of them at once from a flea market or some second-hand store, knowing he'd send them over time.

After eyeballing the images a little longer, Connor decided they yielded nothing of value, or at least no value he could understand at the moment. Perhaps later, after uncovering some presently unknown breadcrumb, a connection would be more evident.

Next, Connor examined the canceled postage stamps on each card. They had all been cancelled on the same day each year—June 7th, the day of the murders. That showed a deliberateness in the timing. The sender had either dropped the postcards off at a mail drop first thing in the morning each year on June 7th, so as to not miss the pickup that day, or hand-delivered them to a post office.

After studying the dated cancellation stamps, Connor arranged the postcards in the order Little Freddie had received them, going back to 2009. He carefully taped them on the wall next to the map, then marked the pink circles on the map with a number representing the order they arrived. He was looking for a pattern. Perhaps the timeline revealed an obvious route across the country.

Connor stepped back and looked at the sequence. Completely random. The first card came from San Diego and the second from Tampa, then Lincoln and then New York, and so on. There didn't seem to be an obvious pattern to the order, which prompted Connor to think of two scenarios. One, the sender visited these cities to mail the cards himself, or, two, he sent them to another individual who was making the drop in those cities.

Given they referenced two explicit murders, it would be risky for the killer to send the postcards to someone else to mail. The sender couldn't risk someone taking them to the police or exposing them in another way. Connor assumed the killer was sending the cards himself, but that meant traveling all over the country. Seemed like a lot of effort to mail a single postcard. Another option was the killer had a job that took him to these cities, and he mailed the cards while he was there. That's a hefty business travel schedule.

If Little Freddie had gone to the police, they would have dusted the postcards for prints and hoped to get something they could match to a database. Several people likely touched each of the cards as they made the journey to Little Freddie's home. The police would be able to cross-reference the prints with the postal employees, and bingo, whoever was left was the likely sender. Connor could dust for prints, but he'd have no way to check his findings against a database and link a print to a name. They don't give that kind of access to ex-military intelligence officers working for criminals. He also had no way of removing the postal employees from the suspect pool.

Fingerprints were out.

Surveillance was another option. If the sender dropped off the postcards at the post office, which would be a logical step to ensure the postcards were postmarked on the specific date, there could be surveillance footage of him making the drop. The problem with footage was that some post offices don't keep their video archives for very long. While Connor may be able to get the footage from the most recent mailing —via some creative means—getting video footage from a drop two years or more ago would likely not happen.

The most recent postcard arrived from Cody, Wyoming. Cody is a small town and probably only had one post office, so getting surveillance footage from that location could be an option. But a positive ID would depend on getting a clear look at what everyone was bringing inside the building. That might be easy for a parcel, but not for a small piece of mail. If the sender was careful, and all evidence suggested he was, he never stepped foot inside the post office. He could have used a mailbox in the post office parking lot, grocery store, or even an office building lobby.

Video surveillance was out.

This would be a difficult case to solve, but Connor didn't solve easy cases. People came to him when they couldn't go to the police or other investigators couldn't get the job done. This case presented a slew of roadblocks, speed bumps, and hurdles, but there was a way through. Connor had to find it.

Two factors would guide his investigation. The first was his assumption the sender was mailing the postcards himself and traveling to these cities to mail them instead of sending them to a proxy. The second factor was that there was a connection between these cities. They weren't random. There was a pattern. It just wasn't obvious yet.

If he wasn't a casual traveler and was city-hopping for business, he traveled a lot to be in a different city every June 7th. More than just a meeting here or there, this guy was on the road all the time. It was part of his job description, which meant he could be in construction, hospitality, events, long-haul trucking, or something related.

Connor stepped away from the map and went to the kitchen for a can of root beer. He decided to go down to the dock to clear his head. The map could wait. Cracking open the can, he looked across the lake. It was nearing dusk, and the skyline was awash with orange and yellow hues. Night came quickly this far east, and it would be dark within the hour. Except for a lone fishing boat, there was no traffic on the lake. A loon called out somewhere nearby. Connor kicked open the folding chair, sat down, and set his gaze on the Maine sky.

He didn't want to think about Little Freddie's postcards anymore today. There would be plenty of time tomorrow.

5

SAVAGE SEASON

SUMMERING at a lake house in the middle of nowhere, Maine, was well suited for relaxing, fishing, and day drinking, but it made doing anything else difficult. Albert, Connor's father, still owned the island property and refused any modern amenities except electricity, indoor plumbing, and a washing machine. Albert always told Connor, "If you want cable television, Internet, or air conditioning, stay in Boston." Usually, Connor had no trouble parting with these luxuries while on the island, even enjoyed it, but these days, investigating anything without an Internet connection was approaching impossible.

The library in Calais, Maine, was an option. It rented computers by the hour, but that was a forty-five-minute drive. The other option was a few hundred yards away.

Thomas Savage, the CEO of a steel company in North Carolina, bought the five-acre island next to Albert's island twenty-some years ago. Lore said Henry Ford was the original owner. He built a wilderness estate on the grounds, complete with a main house, four servant cabins, and a cabin for his personal boat captain. The island changed hands multiple times over the years, finally ending up with Thomas Savage. All of the original structures were still there, but the main house was the only one Thomas kept up.

Albert always told stories about how he, Thomas, and Mitch Skinner would stay up all night getting drunk and playing poker. That all stopped when Thomas married Tara, a divorce attorney half his age, who then accompanied him to the island each summer.

Thomas always said Tara was an excellent divorce attorney. Connor learned that firsthand two years ago when Thomas got caught having an affair. Tara filed the divorce paperwork the next day. Of all his assets, the island in the middle of Meddybemps Lake was the only thing Thomas wanted in the divorce, which is why his wife fought so hard to get it. Tara Savage lived up to her name.

Savage Island, as it came to be known, had everything a summer home could ask for, including high-speed Internet. Thomas had paid to run the cables across the lake bottom years ago.

As Connor sipped his morning coffee on the dock, he watched Savage Island. A US flag attached to the boathouse flapped in the breeze, signaling to the rest of the islanders that someone was there. The vacationers always lowered their flags for the summer, but Tara's had been waving unapologetically since Connor arrived at the Harding cabin two weeks ago.

Halfway into his second cup of coffee, movement across the lake caught his eye. Tara had come down to one of her four docks. It was the first time Connor had seen her this year. He reached for the binoculars he kept on the dock and squinted through them. Tara wore an orange swimsuit, which was brighter than the morning sun, black sunglasses, and a white sun hat. The hat was oversized. The orange two-piece wasn't. She laid a blanket across the dock and sat down with her legs crossed. Then she grabbed a book with one hand and a margarita with the other. When she looked up and saw Connor on his dock, she tipped her glass in his direction.

After polishing off the rest of his coffee, he returned to the cabin to retrieve his notebook and went to fire up the pontoon boat. The engine gurgled and spat out a frothy wake as he backed away from the dock. He kept his speed low, not wanting to shatter the quiet stillness of the morning. Tara watched curiously as he inched closer to her dock. He cut the engine when he was twenty or so feet away and let the lake carry him in.

"Morning," he said. "Still castrating ex-husbands?"

"Only those who deserve it." She removed her sunglasses. Her long black hair reached her ribcage. She was tan, almost too tan, and had a body that could sell magazines.

"What brings you over here, Connor?"

"You working up here?"

"Working vacation. I'll be here for a few more weeks."

"I was hoping to use your computer and Internet."

"Is that what passes for a pick-up line out here? Internet access?"

"It's not a line. I need to do some research, and I don't want to go all the way to Calais."

"Looking up nursing homes for your asshole father I hope."

He swallowed a laugh. "Something like that."

27

She set down her book and glass, walked to the edge of the dock, and tossed Connor a line. It landed square in his hand.

"Is that a yes?" asked Connor.

She pulled the pontoon boat close. When it budged the dock, she handed Connor the slack and went back to her blanket.

"Computer is already on in the office," she said. "Blender is in the kitchen if you want to help yourself to a drink."

"Thanks. I won't be long." He grabbed his notebook, tied off the boat, and followed the rocky path through the woods to the main house.

The path led to the wraparound front porch, which smelled of pine. Connor crossed the porch, opened the screen door, and stepped inside. It had been a few years since Connor had been inside, but it was just as he remembered it. The living room was massive; Connor figured he could fit his entire cabin inside. Two large stone fireplaces faced each other on opposite sides of the room. The home was meant for entertaining, although Connor couldn't remember it being used that way for a long time, at least not while he was up in Maine. He recalled five or so years ago, when Thomas and Tara were still married, they hosted an island party for everyone on the lake that summer. Now, it felt like a castle for one.

He stepped through the living room to a hallway that led to the office. It was a small room with pine walls and a built-in desk, also pine. The desk looked original to the room, and he wondered if Henry Ford had ever worked there. The laptop was already on, as Tara had said. Connor sat down, pulled it toward him, opened his notebook and got to work.

He didn't have the traditional law enforcement resources to rely on. Instead, he'd apply his own dime-store psycho-analysis to identify the person on the other end of the postcards.

He was convinced the locations the sender mailed the postcards from were not random at all. He also figured the sender traveled for a living and was mailing the cards from whatever city his travels took him to each June 7th. Of all the jobs that kept a potential killer on the road, trucker seemed the most obvious. It was also the most cliche, but it was cliche for a reason. It happens all the time.

Trucking companies fall into a few categories, including regional and national. Given how spread out the cities were, if the sender worked as a trucker, he'd be working for a national carrier. There was also a chance he was an independent trucker who planned his own routes, but even independent truckers tend to work for the same customers and run the same routes. It's more profitable that way.

Connor spent the next few hours on various trucking associations and trucking company websites compiling a list of every trucking company that serviced the postcard cities. If he could narrow down the list of companies delivering to all the cities, he could try to find a way to identify the drivers on those routes. And if he could find drivers with active routes to those cities the postcards were mailed from, he'd have a solid suspect list.

It was a stretch, and he wasn't sure how he would get a driver list from the trucking companies, but he'd cross that bridge when he came to it. *If* he came to it. A trucker was still a shot in the dark.

He cross-referenced his list of trucking companies with the list of cities and shook his head. Most of the national companies hit the big burgs, but none of them delivered to all of them. Of all the trucking companies in the US, All-Ride Logistics hit the most cities, but even they only delivered to seventy-five percent of the targets.

Truckers leave companies all the time, and it's likely the driver wasn't with the same company for the past twelve years. Perhaps he worked for one, which serviced certain cities, then moved to another, maybe several other companies, which serviced the other towns.

To follow up on that theory, Connor further segmented his list to see if he could identify a timeline where a trucker could have hopped companies and still hit all the cities. Was there a combination of trucking companies that serviced all the areas? Another hour and he had his answer. Had a driver worked for four different companies on Connor's list, he could have hit all of the cities except one. Cody, Wyoming. Cody was only reachable by using smaller trucking companies, which would pick up freight from a warehouse after a larger company dropped it off. No matter how he sliced it, Connor couldn't conjure up a scenario in which someone driving for these companies could have been in each of these cities on June 7th over the past twelve years.

His eyes were glazing over when Tara appeared in the doorway holding two beers and wearing a white beach coverup.

"You suck at taking vacations," she said, handing him a

can. "I think there's a law up here that you can't work more than two hours a day on the lake."

"I haven't been working that long." He looked at his wrist and noticed the missing watch.

"You've been in here for six hours."

"Six hours?"

"I was going to offer you lunch a few hours ago, but you looked too into something, and I didn't want to bother you."

"I didn't realize I'd been here that long."

"It's no problem, but now I'm kicking you out of my house. You can join me on the dock for a beer as thanks for the computer."

Connor looked at his notebook and realized how much work he'd done. It was a solid start for a man on vacation.

"I could do that."

"Oh, fuck off. Don't make it sound like a chore." She walked through the living room and down to the dock. Connor packed up his notebook and followed her.

She adjusted her sun hat and eased into a deck chair. Connor took the one next to her.

"So, what are you working on anyway?" she asked.

"Nothing interesting."

"I know you're some type of investigator. I ran into your father last summer at Palmer's. He was drunk off his ass and wouldn't shut up about you."

Connor cracked open the beer. "That checks out."

"So, what is it?"

"A client of mine, he's receiving threatening letters in the mail. I'm trying to figure out who's sending them."

"Why doesn't he go to the police?"

"My clients don't go to the police." Connor turned the

red-and-white beer can in his hand. It was Belfast Bay Lobster Ale.

Only in Maine.

"You're in the private investigation business?"

Connor squinted in the afternoon soon. "No. I'm in the getting shit done business."

"I've got a few people like that at my firm."

"Those the guys with cameras catching all those ex-husbands with their pants down?"

"They do other things too. Whatever they have to do to get the job done."

"I know the type."

"Is your father coming back up here this summer? I saw your brother and his family up here last month."

"No, Albert's done for the summer. Just me."

"You like it over there alone?"

"I'm used to being alone. I prefer it that way."

"I prefer to be alone too," she said. "Most of the time."

Connor looked back at the main house. "This is a huge place. You could get lost in there."

"I only ever go into maybe three rooms. The rest of it is wasted space. I fell in love with it up here, though. It was the one positive thing Thomas brought to our marriage. Now, I can't get out of the city fast enough. Life is just different here."

"Got that right."

Connor finished his beer and looked across the lake at the empty deck chair on his own dock. "Thanks for the office space and the hospitality." He stood up. "I've got to get back. More work to do."

"The office is yours whenever you need it. Just come

over. If I'm not here, the door will be unlocked. It's nice to talk to someone. That's the only bad thing about being up here alone. I miss talking to people."

Connor knew the feeling.

"You know, Tara, you're not nearly as insufferable as my father made you out to be."

"He just hates me because he was friends with Thomas and he's pissed about me taking this place."

"I reckon you're right."

She stood up and started toward the main house. "Reckon all you want, Connor. Don't be a stranger."

Connor watched as she walked through the wooded path to the house. He gathered his notes, fired up the boat, untied the line, and pointed the wheel toward his own place.

6

THE CALAIS LIBRARY

THE TRUCKING ANGLE WAS A BUST. That's what Connor thought when he went to bed, and he still agreed when he woke up. After a breakfast of two granola bars and three cups of coffee, he decided it was time to get out of Meddybemps for a while. Grabbing his boat keys and flip-flops, he went down to the lake. Across the water, he saw Tara sunning herself on her dock. She wore the same white sun hat but had exchanged the bright orange two-piece for a black one. He waved, but she didn't wave back. Her eyes must be closed under that wide-brimmed hat. That's what Connor thought.

He fired up the engine and tore across the lake. The shortest route to Mitch Skinner's dock was through the narrow channel between two unnamed islands off the south end of the boathouse. But it hadn't rained in a week and the lake was low. Craggy stone tendrils, usually concealed by the water, broke the surface, daring Connor to try the narrows. He refused, instead taking the longer route around the most dangerous spots.

Ten minutes later, he arrived at Mitch's dock. His old friend was usually outside tackling a dock repair, clearing brush, or doing something else to stave off boredom. Today, though, his property was quiet. Connor exchanged the pontoon boat for his Jeep Wrangler and navigated the narrow driveway leading from Mitch's property out to Stone Road and then to Route 191. He took 191 to Route 1 and rolled into Calais, Maine, forty minutes later.

The Calais Library sat on a hill overlooking the town. It had two floors. The main one housed the general stacks, while the lower lever had a small computer lab on one side and a children's craft area on the other.

He stopped at the front desk in the computer lab and slid his driver's license, required currency to rent a computer at the Calais Library, across to the counter to the clerk. She was young, maybe early twenties, and looked like she didn't want to be there.

"Connor Harding?" she said, reading his license.

"That's right. I want to rent a computer for a few hours."

"You related to Albert Harding?"

Connor considered his answer carefully. "He's my father."

She chomped her gum, yanked a printout from behind the counter, and showed it to Connor. "*This* Albert Harding?"

It was a photocopy of Albert's driver's license. Above the image, someone had written NO COMPUTER ACCESS in large black letters.

"I can only imagine what you caught him looking at," said Connor.

She tapped Connor's license against the scuffed countertop.

"Look," said Connor. "We share the same DNA, not the same Internet interests. I'm just here to look for a job."

The sympathy angle worked. The young clerk tucked his license into a clear pocket on the back of a binder and handed him a Post-it note with a four-digit login code.

"Number one," she said. "And keep it clean."

"Right." Connor grabbed the code, took a seat across the room at one of the six PCs, and went to work.

He had abandoned the trucking idea, which meant he had to find another reason someone would have been in those twelve cities on June 7th. He wasn't sure why, but his brain steered him toward corporate trade shows. He'd never had a corporate job, and the US Army wasn't keen on sending their intelligence officers to conferences, but Connor knew they were big business, especially in certain industries.

He turned to a fresh page in his notebook and made a list of all the main conference venues in the target cities. His strategy was to look at each venue and see what previous events they hosted on June 7th. If he could find any consistent events that traveled to these cities, he might have something.

He abandoned that line of investigation an hour later when it was apparent there was no link. A few of the smaller cities on the list didn't even have venues large enough to host an event.

The one piece missing from this investigation was the human element. When he'd worked for US Army Intelligence, he had access to a variety of resources, but information gathered via interpersonal contact was often the most valuable. This type of research was slow and, so far, yielded little for his trouble. Connor preferred having someone to knock around. It was quicker. With less sitting. But there was no one to interrogate, no one to talk to, because aside from Little Freddie, there was no one else at this party.

After abandoning conferences as the possible connection, Connor took another track. He looked for companies that had operations in each of the cities. Maybe whoever was behind the postcards was working for a company and traveled from one field office to another.

He started with the smallest cities first to see what companies had branches there and then extended the search to identify common links. He came close and even got excited once or twice. There was a grocery store chain that serviced nearly all of the cities on the list, except two. But like the trucking angle, could someone hop enough jobs to visit all of these cities? Of course they could. Search long enough, and he would find some correlation, whether two jobs, four jobs, or ten. There were too many variables, and he was spinning his wheels with little to show for it.

"Four-hour limit," said the clerk behind the library counter.

The time had gone by fast. Connor had exhausted his lines of investigation and was eager to get back to the island to regroup. There was something there, he just wasn't seeing it. Not yet, but solving a case like this was like trudging through a swamp. One step after another, and eventually, you get to the other side. Connor wasn't anywhere near the other side. He still had a lot of work to do, but he wasn't going to do it here.

He thanked the clerk and exchanged the slip of paper with the computer code for his driver's license. He fought the urge to ask why Albert was banned from the Calais Library computers. Some things are better left unknown.

Returning to his Jeep, he tossed the notepad on the floor and retraced his route back to Meddybemps.

7

A SINKING FEELING

CONNOR HAD COME to Maine for vacation, not to work. Meddybemps Lake has some of the best smallmouth bass fishing in the country, but right now, Connor wasn't fishing for smallmouth bass. He was fishing for a connection between one individual and twelve cities. His brother had made the mistake of getting under Little Freddie's thumb, and now Connor had to extricate him from that predicament. He wouldn't ask Finn how he ended up owing Freddie. It didn't matter. All that mattered was family. And while it stung a bit now to give up his vacation, in time that sting would pass, and Connor would forget all about the time he helped his brother out of another bad situation. Until, at some family function down the road, Connor would remind him.

Besides his father's questionable Internet habits, Connor's research at the Calais Library had turned up nothing of value. It did let Connor tick off another line of investigation from his list. The trucking, conventions, and corporate travel angles had faded, but what did that leave?

He wasn't sure. He was certain, however, that he was out of alcohol.

He also wanted to relax a bit—he was still on vacation after all. He could kill both those birds at Palmer's. He'd grab dinner there and hope Jack Palmer had a bottle of Scotch he'd be willing to part with. While Palmer didn't sell Scotch at his grocery store, he'd have one or two bottles behind the bar, and he'd been known to sell them if asked nicely.

Dusk settled over Meddybemps as Connor tied off at the town dock. He didn't need his boat lights on the trip to town, but he'd need them on the way back to the island. Night came fast here.

Walking the path to Palmer's, he looked forward to catching up with Jack. Butter him up for a bit, and he was more likely to part with that bottle.

There were about a dozen people at the bar when Connor arrived. For a town like Meddybemps, that was considered busy. He recognized nearly everyone. Summer here long enough, and you got to know the townies. The only two people he didn't recognize were the men at the far booth. You can't know everyone.

Connor dismissed a booth in favor of the bar. Jack poured a glass of well Scotch and set it on a napkin in front of him. Connor's go-to brand was The Balvenie Caribbean Cask, but Jack didn't sell that here. Too fancy, he said.

"Eat'n today?" asked Jack.

"Clams?"

"Fresh out. The chicken salad is gravy, though."

"That on a bun?"

Jack nodded.

"Let's go with that."

Jack returned with the meal a few minutes later, and for the next hour, Connor's head got steadily more cloudy. A rotating cast of characters joined him at the bar, eager to swap fishing stories and talk about the massive turtle that lived in the lake. The locals called it Nessie. Connor saw it last summer when it swam underneath his boat. It was the size of a dishwasher.

One by one, the locals came and went, and Connor found himself alone after Fred Roland and Ben Blankenship headed for home. He wasn't alone for long. Two men approached and sat next to him, one on each side. They were the two unknowns he'd noticed when he arrived. He got the impression they weren't there to talk.

"You a celebrity or something?" asked the man with the large US Marine tattoo on his forearm. The image of a combat knife and the words "Semper Fi" extended from his elbow to his wrist.

"No," said Connor. "If you're looking for celebrities, you're on the wrong coast."

"Just seems everyone around here knows you," said the other man.

"Small town. We know each other. But I don't know you."

"You're Connor Harding, right?" asked the man with the tattoo.

Connor took a sip of his drink. "Cut the shit. Tell me what you want so I can go back to not talking to you."

"How long you on vacation fer," asked the other man.

Connor didn't look at him. "As long as I want."

"You at the house all by yourself? Anyone with you?" The man with the tattoo squeezed his fist, tightening his forearm and making the knife twitch.

Connor worked with bad people and being around murderers, thugs, and other degenerates was as common as brushing his teeth. There were only a few things in this world that rattled him. Ex-Marines flexing their muscles wasn't one of them.

"If there's a point to this conversation, then make it," said Connor. "Otherwise, take a walk."

"You a tough guy?" asked the man to Connor's left.

"Tough enough."

These two ringers weren't from town, that much was obvious. Why they were here was still an unknown. No one knew Connor was in Maine besides Little Freddie and his stocky sidekick. He didn't like people knowing where he was, especially when he was in the middle of nowhere. Albert left a wake of pissed-off people wherever he went, so there was a possibility whoever these two were they were here because of something Albert did. Most people up here knew Connor was Albert's son, and the idea that someone would want to get to Albert through Connor wasn't crazy.

"You should be careful," said the man with the tattoo. "It sure is dark out on that lake, and you're knocking back a lot of drink there. Hope you can make it back home safely."

Connor looked at the man's clenched fist. He was ready to throw a punch, but Connor would beat him to it. He had a few drinks in him and he was outnumbered, but two things would play to his favor. One, the barstools at Palmer's were as rickety as a one-legged ladder, and two, alcohol wasn't the only thing Jack kept behind the bar.

Connor set his drink on the bar and slid it away from him. Looking into the bar mirror, he sized up both men. He'd handle the big man, the one with the tattoo, first. The other man's body language wasn't projecting a fight. Connor moved quick. He grabbed the Marine's collar and jerked backward. The barstool tipped onto two legs, balanced for a moment, and then went over. Before the Marine hit the ground, Connor had already buried his fist into the other man's jaw, cracking at least one bone. He caught him square with the knuckles of his index and middle fingers, his elbow bent at 90 degrees. By the time the Marine got to his feet, he was staring down the barrel of Jack's twelve-gauge. Connor stepped over the man with the broken jaw and moved out of the way in case Jack decided to unload.

"Time to git, fellas," said Jack, struggling against the shotgun's weight.

The two men thought for a moment, considering their options. Once they realized they only had one, they collected themselves and reluctantly walked out of the bar. Jack eyeballed the two grainy, black-and-white security monitors covering the grocery store and parking lot. Once they drove away, he stashed the shotgun back behind the bar.

"What the hell was that about?" asked Jack.

"I was hoping you knew."

Jack shook his head as Connor sat down and retrieved his nearly empty glass from the bar. After Jack refilled it, a familiar face righted the stool next to him and sat down.

"You sure seem to know how to attract trouble," said Tara.

"I get that from my father."

"He do," agreed Jack. He wiped the bar in front of her and disappeared to check on the grocery store.

"Was all that related to that thing you're working on?" asked Tara.

"Not sure. There aren't too many people who know what I've been up to."

"Looks like whoever hired you has some explaining to do then."

"Got that right." Connor watched Tara in the mirror. She wore a black dress that was part business and part not. Her black hair was pulled back into a tight ponytail.

"A bit overdressed for Palmer's, aren't you?"

She looked at Connor's red and black flannel shirt and jeans. "Maybe you're underdressed."

"That's a distinct possibility." His words ran together, and his tongue felt fat in his mouth.

For the next hour and a half, they both got drunk. Connor continued with whatever passed for Scotch, while Tara tossed back several gin and tonics. The next time Connor glanced up in the bar mirror, he noticed they were the only ones left in the room. Jack returned a few minutes later and clicked off the main lights. The two small ceiling lights illuminating the bar stayed on.

"Sorry, you two," said Jack. "You don't have to go home, but you can't stay here."

Connor and Tara stood up. For Connor, it took more effort than usual. Tara headed for the door and Connor followed. He stopped, then walked behind the bar, remembering why he had come to Palmer's in the first place. He held up a bottle of Dewar's.

"Hey, Jack, can you part with this?"

"I reckon so. I'll add it to your tab. Now git the hell out of here so's I can lock up and go home."

Connor double-timed it out the front door, struggling to keep his balance. When he arrived in the gravel parking lot, Tara was waiting for him.

"Walk me back to the dock?" she asked.

"Of course."

They navigated the path from Palmer's to the town dock, the alcohol and the darkness working against them. They arrived at the dock and found the only two boats moored there were Connor's pontoon boat and Tara's vintage mahogany Chris-Craft. Connor squinted to read the name printed in black letters on the stern. F. U. MONEY.

"Nice touch," he said.

He started to walk her toward her boat, but she stopped.

"I'd rather take yours." She leaned in and kissed his neck. Her breath smelled like pine needles.

He wrapped his arm around her waist, led her to his boat, and helped her aboard. She fired the engine while he struggled to untie the blurry knot from the dock's cleat. When he finally untied it, he jumped onto the boat, nearly losing his balance.

He took the wheel and knocked the throttle forward, spitting the wake up over the dock. Tara continued to kiss his neck, and Connor fought the alcohol-induced fog and the choppy waves, trying to remember the safest route back to his island.

They had only been on the water for a few minutes when a bright spotlight blinded him.

"What the hell is that?" said Tara.

Connor instinctively cut the engine and braced his eyes against the light. He heard what he thought was a shotgun racking, and then someone yelled.

"Now!"

Sensing what was coming next, Connor grabbed the back of Tara's dress and leaped over the starboard side. They hit the water as the first blast tore into the pontoon boat. Connor pulled her under and kicked away from the vessel. The water was cold, the kind of cold that sobers you up on impact. As he swam, several large rocks tore into Connor's ribs. He felt Tara push off of him and head to the surface for air. He followed, and when they broke the surface, they were some fifty feet away from the boat. Several more blasts shattered the quiet night. The next series of shots hit the gas tank, and the back half of the boat exploded.

Connor turned and noticed they weren't far from Blumheart's Island. He pulled Tara close.

"Can you get to that island?"

She nodded.

"Stay under for as long as you can."

She nodded again and disappeared into the inky water. Connor inhaled, closed his eyes, and dove under. He came up every ten seconds to check if the other boat was following them. A few minutes later, Connor and Tara pulled themselves onto Peter Blumheart's dock. Connor looked back to see the bright spotlight scanning the surface of the lake. The front part of Connor's boat bobbed in the water, likely held up by an underwater boulder.

"Your friends from the bar?" asked Tara.

"Suppose so."

Connor pulled her close and she shivered into him. "You seem pretty calm for a person who just went through that."

"So do you," she said.

"It's not my first time."

Blumheart's island was completely dark, and Connor led Tara up the wooden steps to the main cabin. Connor knew Peter was staying with his daughter in Connecticut for the summer. He also knew he kept a spare key under the rear leg of the front porch table.

Connor slid the table to the side, grabbed the key, and opened the door. They watched from the bedroom window as the spotlight swept across the lake. A few minutes later, the light went out and they heard the motor gurgle and the boat slowly fade away in the distance.

"You think they'll come back?"

"Not tonight. With an explosion like that, someone's already called the police. They won't risk being on the water if someone shows up."

Fighting the chills, Connor rummaged through Blumheart's closet, removed an oversized sweatshirt, and tossed it on the floor at Tara's feet.

"Get out of that wet dress before you freeze to death."

She peeled off the dress and tossed it over the bedroom door. Then she pushed Connor onto the bed, ignoring the sweatshirt on the floor.

Connor woke to the morning sun warming his face. It took a moment before he remembered where he was. When he rolled to his side, Tara was gone. He sat up and took in the room. The queen-sized bed filled most of the room. There was a small white nightstand with a digital clock that had been unplugged. A quilt hung on the wall next to the closet door. Windows offering a clear view of the lake lined the opposite wall.

After he rolled out of bed, Connor retrieved his flannel shirt and jeans from atop the bedroom door. They were still damp when he slipped them on. While Tara was long gone, her dress remained. Connor swiped the dress, made the bed, and erased any evidence they were ever there.

He searched the rustic cabin for Tara, but there was no trace of her. He closed the front door, locked it, and returned the key beneath the table leg. As he made his way down to the dock, he looked out over the lake. An aluminum pontoon bobbed in the water where the rest of his boat had gone down. A few white hull fragments floated about, but the rest his boat was lost to the murky lake bottom, along with Jack's bottle of Scotch.

He was surveying the damage when the hum of a boat motor drifted in from the east. He turned to find the F.U. MONEY darting toward him. When she was forty feet out, Tara killed the engine and drifted in to Blumheart's dock.

"Morning, sunshine," she said.

"How did you get back to the dock?"

"Four years swimming for Columbia University."

"You swam that?"

Her hands were shaking, but she winked and waved him onboard.

"Those guys coming back?" she asked, looking over her shoulder.

"Depends."

"On what?"

"On whether they were hired to scare me or kill me."

"Do you want to go to the police?"

"No. Take me back to my place so I can get out of these wet clothes."

"Then what?"

"Then I'm going hunting."

She threw the throttle forward and tore away from Blumheart's island. She didn't speak again until they arrived at Connor's dock. When Connor climbed out, Tara looked over her shoulder again.

"Don't worry," said Connor. "You're safe."

"Like hell I am."

"They're long gone."

"What if they come back? I'm over there all by myself."

"They came for me," said Connor. "They won't know who you are. Besides, I'm going into town to find them."

"What am I supposed to do? This may be a common occurrence for you, but not me."

"What, a client's pissed-off husband never shotgunned your boat into oblivion?"

"Not funny, Connor."

"You're right. I'm sorry. Can you give me a few minutes to change and then drop me off at Mitch Skinner's place? Then maybe you could get out of town for a bit. Maybe head into Acadia."

She nodded, and Connor ran up the mossy path to the main cabin. Inside, he changed out of his wet clothes, grabbed his .45 and cell phone from the dresser and tucked them inside his gray backpack. When he returned to the dock, Tara was changing into a coverall she had stashed somewhere on the boat. Her hands were still shaking.

"You okay?" asked Connor.

"I'll be fine. Just amped up at the moment."

"It'll fade."

She nodded and fired up the boat.

When Tara dropped Connor off at Mitch Skinner's place, she looked eager to get the hell out of there. He wondered if he'd see her again when he got back from town. He hoped to, but something told him she would be gone when he returned.

8

THE MAN IN THE MERCEDES

THE HARDING FAMILY rented two parking spots from Mitch Skinner each summer. They were on the edge of his property next to a weathered shed that looked like it could go at any minute. One space was for the pontoon boat trailer. At the end of every summer, Connor paid to have the pontoon hauled out and sent to Moose Island Marine in Eastport, Maine, for winter storage. Every spring, the marina delivered the boat back to the lake so it was waiting for the family when they arrived.

Connor's Jeep occupied the other space. The nearby trees kept the vehicle cool, but the shade also meant Connor had to deal with a barrage of mosquitoes every time he returned to the Jeep. It was a race to get into the vehicle and close the door before a battalion of bloodsuckers slipped in.

After making his way to Skinner's dock and inside the vehicle, he took his cell phone from his backpack and checked for a signal. It was faint, but it would work. He dialed and waited. It rang several times before the call connected.

"You got a name for me yet?" asked Little Freddie.

"No, but I was hoping you'd have two for me."

"I don't follow."

"I had a run-in with two asshats in town last night. They didn't tell me what they wanted, but it was obvious they were here to rattle me."

"And?"

"And they blew my boat to shit."

"Why are you calling me about it?"

"It was obvious they were here to send me a message. Perhaps to stop looking into your postcard murderer. Who else knows what I'm doing?"

"No one. Is there a chance you're getting close to a name? Maybe someone got nervous. Could be a good sign."

"First, it's never a good sign when someone sinks your boat. Second, I'm nowhere near close. I've got nothing on your murderer, so no one is getting nervous. But maybe you talked to someone about what I'm doing, or maybe Boone talked. Someone doesn't like what I'm up to, and they didn't find out about it from me."

"Look, I don't talk about my business with anyone."

"Somebody knows," said Connor, "and I aim to find out who and how."

He clicked the phone off.

A moment later, Boone answered his ringing cell phone.

"Two men went after Connor last night," said Little Freddie.

"Who?"

"Don't know, but look into it. Connor didn't recognize them, so they must be from out of town."

"I'll see what I can dig up."

"No one gets in Connor's way on this," said Little Freddie. "Find out who it was and make sure they won't be a problem again."

"I'm on it."

Meddybemps was a small town, and while it had an overabundance of charm and bait shops, one thing it didn't have was a motel. The nearest one of those was in Calais, up the street from the library. It was the only motel within a thirty-mile radius. Connor hoped the two men he met at Palmer's were staying there.

He pulled out of Skinner's dirt driveway onto Stone Road and then onto 191. A black Mercedes started tailing him a quarter-mile later. Connor had assumed Little Freddie would keep him on a short leash, but he hadn't expected it to be this short.

When Connor arrived at the Motorway Inn in Calais, there were only two cars in the parking lot. Both had Maine plates. The woman working the front desk looked happy to see someone, but Connor knew she would have been happy to see anyone.

"Checking in?"

"No."

The woman looked disappointed.

"I'm looking for two men and thought they might be staying here. They were both about my height. One had a buzzcut. Dark skinned, maybe Mexican. Had a tattoo of a knife on his forearm. Looked like an asshole."

"The other guy have slick-backed hair? White guy?"

"That's right," said Connor. "They staying here?"

"Were staying here. They checked out this morning."

"You have any idea where they went?"

"No. They had Maine plates, though." The woman dug into her pocket and pulled out a cell phone with a cracked screen. "I asked them to fill out the ledger, but they refused." She tapped on the worn book on the counter. "We're supposed to get a name and license plate number."

"You get their names?"

"No. When I asked them to fill out the ledger they told me to fuck off. I thought that was rude. I figured they didn't want me to know who they were, so I got a photo of their license plate. Just in case."

"Can I see the photo?"

She tapped the cracked screen, pulled up the image, and showed it to Connor, who wrote it down on a piece of paper.

"They also stunk up the place. It's a no smoking room, but they didn't care. Now, I have to get the carpets cleaned. It reeks in there."

"Sorry to hear that. If I find them, I'll be sure to mention it."

"You a cop or something?"

"Or something." Connor thanked her, slid a fifty-dollar bill across the counter, and returned to the parking lot to find the Mercedes parked next to his Jeep. The driver's window lowered as he approached. Inside was Little Freddie's muscle, the one who had been wedged into Mitch Skinner's rented canoe days earlier.

"You following me?" asked Connor.

"Freddie said you had some visitors last night."

"You know anything about that?"

Boone shook his head. "What did you learn in the motel?"

"Maine plates. I plan to find them and get to the bottom of it."

"Why don't you let me do that? You got other things to worry about."

"No thanks. I like solving my own problems. Besides, I'm not convinced this leak didn't come from your organization."

"It didn't come from us. We're on your side here."

Connor stared him down.

"Give me the plate," said Boone. "I can find these two in a few hours. I'll give you the names and you can do whatever you like with them. Right now, we need you on Freddie's case."

Connor didn't like someone else looking into this, but he also knew his resources were limited. If Boone could find the two men from last night, why not let him? It was obvious they were leaving town anyway, and Connor didn't have the time to chase them. He needed to focus on making headway on the postcards.

"Fine." Connor snapped a photo of the scrap paper before handing it through the open window.

"What did they look like?"

Connor described every detail he could remember.

"I'll find them."

"The postcards your boss gave me aren't giving me much to work with. When you find these two, I want to know who sent them. If they're connected to this investigation, then that's going to be the best way to find whoever sent the postcards."

"How do I get ahold of you? You said there was no phone service on your island."

Connor jotted down a phone number. "This is Mitch's landline. Call him if you have anything. He can get a message to me."

When Connor returned to his parking spot, the mosquitoes and Mitch Skinner were waiting for him.

"Heard you had a fun night," said Mitch. "Who did it?"

"Don't know. But I aim to find out. You hear anything about it?"

"Just that you're in the market for a new boat." He pointed to the old Boston Whaler with the sun-bleached canopy tied to the dock. "I'll sell you that one."

"Not looking to buy, but I'll rent it for a few days."

"It's yours for as long as you need it. Keys and gas are in it."

Connor thanked him and headed toward the boat, leaving his old friend and the mosquitoes behind.

9

LEAVING ON A JET PLANE

THE BOSTON WHALER bounced across the choppy lake as Connor headed back to his family's cabin. The route took him around several islands, including Tara's complex. After seeing the F. U. MONEY moored in the boathouse, he slowed down and turned toward her dock.

Stepping onto the wooden planks, he found the deck chairs that had been scattered about a day earlier were now neatly stacked near a tree. The towels were gone and the flag no longer hung on the pole.

Connor jogged up the path to find Tara standing on the front porch. She was wearing jeans and a long-sleeve button-up shirt. Not dock attire.

"Find what you were looking for in town?" she asked, fidgeting with her hand.

"Still working on it."

"I'm heading back to North Carolina."

"When?"

She checked her watch. "Soon."

"Those guys are gone. No need to cut your vacation short."

"I need to get back to the firm anyway. You know, more ex-husbands to castrate." She managed a smile.

"Need a ride to the mainland?"

"I do, actually. Can you hang out here for a few minutes? I'm almost done packing."

Connor followed her into the house, where she slipped into the bedroom. Connor wanted to follow her and try to convince her to stay, but something told him not to. When she returned to the living room, she rolled two bulky suitcases.

"Need to print something out," she said and disappeared into the office down the hall.

Connor thought about the massive cabin sitting empty for the rest of the summer. Usually, he liked to be alone up here. He liked his routine. He liked not seeing or hearing anyone. But he had gotten used to the idea of seeing Tara on the dock each morning, and the thought of her leaving got to him. Maybe had he not been working on Little Freddie's postcard case, things would have been different and he'd have more time with her. But then again, had it not been for that shoebox of cards, he'd have never needed an Internet connection. Fate is funny that way.

When Tara returned from the office, she dropped a boarding pass on top of her purse.

"You flying out of Bangor?"

"Portland. But I couldn't get a direct flight into Char-lotte. Apparently, today's the one day they don't fly direct. Had to go to through Worcester." She shook her head. "I loathe regional airports. There's never anything good to eat."

She grabbed her suitcase handles. "You ready for that ferry ride?"

He took her suitcases and carried them down to the Boston Whaler. The suitcase wheels skipped across the warped wooden planks. When she settled into the boat, he untied the line and started toward the town dock. The wind had died down and they flew across the still water.

At the dock, he helped her unload the bags and took them to her rental car parked near the back of the lot.

"That case you're working on," she said. "The Internet is all yours. There's a spare key in the toolbox inside the boathouse. Use it whenever you like."

"Thanks. You coming back next summer?"

"Don't know. I like it up here, but it can be tough getting away long enough to enjoy it. We'll have to see."

"I hope you can figure it out," said Connor. "It'd be nice to see you again."

"I don't like getting shot at, Connor. And I feel like, with you, that would be a recurring theme. You know all those stories about women falling for the bad boy? Great for romance novels, but it's horseshit in real life."

"That's not a typical night for me." He smiled.

"I hope not. Goodbye, Connor." She kissed him. He hoped it would have been longer, but it was a kiss from someone trying to make a plane. He went back to the boat and did everything he could not to watch the car roll out of the parking lot.

He was already thinking about Tara on his way back to the island, but not in the way he wanted to think about her. It wasn't about missing her, even though he did. He thought about something she said about her itinerary. How she hated regional airports.

Connor kicked the throttle forward and blew through the narrows. Usually, he'd never risk the shoal, but some newfound confidence propelled him through. He pulled up to his dock, looped the line around the cleat and bolted toward the house. After stuffing his notebook inside his backpack, he returned to the boat and set off for Tara's island.

The spare key was right where she said it was. A few minutes later, he sat in front of her humming PC with his notebook in his lap and a list of regional airports in front of him.

10

PHOTOGRAPHIC EVIDENCE

CONNOR WAS STILL confident that whoever was sending the postcards to Little Freddie had a job that took him across the country. He had come up empty so far, but Tara's airline layover in Worcester gave him a new angle to investigate. Regional airlines service small or lightly-populated areas. Some of those carriers are owned by larger airlines, while others operate independently.

Connor scanned his list of cities and went to work on Tara's PC. After a solid hour of research, he'd discovered two interesting facts. Each of the cities on his list had an airport, and each of those airports had a post office. That meant someone flying to these cities on June 7th each year could mail a postcard and have it stamped with a June 7th date without leaving the terminal. Seemed encouraging, but there were a lot of airline employees crisscrossing the country each day.

The next step was to boil that total down, which meant looking at each postcard city to see which airlines were servicing their airports. Could someone fly to each of these cities while working for the same airline?

He found his answer in Devil's Lake, North Dakota, and then confirmed it in West Yellowstone, Montana. The same regional airline, Trans Air, serviced both of those cities. And the kicker? Trans Air was the *only* airline flying into Devil's Lake and West Yellowstone. That couldn't be a coincidence. Connor expanded his search and found that Trans Air also serviced all of the other regional airports in the smaller cities on his list. He cross-referenced the major metros, New York, San Diego, and Tampa with the airline's route map and found something interesting. All of the major metros were Trans Air hubs.

That meant someone flying for Trans Air could visit each of the postcard cities while on the clock. An additional few hours of research confirmed no other airline hit all twelve of the postcard cities. Not even close.

Connor wasn't a big believer in coincidences, and he was not about to start now. Whoever was sending those cards was a Trans Air employee, and if they were city hopping, that meant they were a pilot or a flight attendant. But how many pilots or flight attendants were moonlighting as contract killers?

Connor knew several pilots from his time in the military who flew for commercial airliners. He knew they had to keep detailed records of their flights for certificate, rating, and instrument proficiency purposes. He recalled one of his pilot friends showing him an official logbook that detailed dates, flight times, and locations of takeoffs and landings. He also remembered seeing flight crew information. It was common to identify the pilot in command, but probably not as essential to detail the flight attendants on board.

The next step would prove a daunting one. Connor had to isolate which crew members were working the Trans Air flights into each of the postcard cities on the days the post-cards were sent, but those records were not publicly available. He assumed the airline kept detailed flight information to comply with FAA requirements. If the FAA wanted to know how many flight hours a specific pilot had behind the yoke of a 727, they needed to confirm it with the airline. He assumed the airline also tracked this information for flight attendants. And that meant records. Reams and reams of records.

He could go to the airline and ask for the information, but that meant impersonating an FBI or FAA investigator. That was serious business and carried a hefty jail term if caught. Connor wasn't about to put that much skin in the game. Not for Little Freddie. A scam like that would also be tough to pull off. Not impossible, but damn near close. If Connor called the airline asking for flight records, the first thing a competent airline employee would do would be to verify his identity. They'd call whatever agency he said he was working for and verify the credentials of whatever name Connor gave them. That play would crumble like a crouton.

The key was to come up with a scenario that was so mundane it wouldn't warrant checking into, and that meant finding a way to get flight crew information without going through the airline. Connor wondered who had access to airline crew records besides the FAA.

. . .

Boone swallowed the last bite of his second chicken sandwich. He was wiping mayo from his fingers when his cell phone rang.

"What you got?" he asked.

"The license plate you gave me. The car is registered to a lumber company outside of Bangor, Maine."

"Lumber company?"

"That's right. I emailed you the address."

"Thanks."

Boone clicked off the phone and returned to his fingers. Satisfied they were clean, he picked up his phone and found the address in his email. He plugged the address into a map app and wiped his mouth with his last napkin.

"Two hours away," he said to himself. He started the engine.

Needing some fresh air, Connor left Tara's office and walked out onto the wraparound deck to think. The weather was perfect. The water was calm, the wind was quiet, and there wasn't a boat motor to be heard. As he walked down to the dock, he thought about what it would be like to travel all the time flying for an airline. He was no stranger to traveling. When he was in US Army Intelligence, he circled the globe more times than he could count, but he usually spent months in the same location. He wasn't a jet-setter. Flight crews could be in three different cities on the same day. And while they got plenty of opportunities to see the world, it still seemed like a brutal way to make a living. Connor couldn't fathom spending all that time away from home and living out of hotels.

That's when it hit him. Hotels. Flight crews stayed in hotels all the time. Not after every flight, but Connor knew the FAA mandated how many hours pilots could fly each day. He figured it was the same for flight attendants. Work them too hard, and they wouldn't be able to safely do their job. So, if they weren't in the air and weren't in their home city, they were staying in a hotel. And if Trans Air was snatching up thousands of hotel rooms every year, that meant they had a corporate contract with certain hotel chains. But which ones?

He went back inside to Tara's office and dialed up a social media site. He entered "Trans Air" into the search window, and after a few minutes of stalking, he had four accounts from Trans Air flight attendants and one from a Trans Air pilot. He scoured all four accounts, but it was Savanna Rose and her prolific photos that gave Connor what he was looking for.

Savanna Rose was a Trans Air flight attendant with a vibrant social media presence. She was young, attractive, and trying desperately to convince her followers that her life was worthy of their eyeballs, clicks, and subscriptions. She posted up to seven times a day, chronicling her adventures across the country with photos of airports, hotspots, other attractive people, and a rare Bible verse tossed in for seasoning.

It wasn't Savanna's photos Connor was interested in, although there were plenty of those to ogle. It was the geotags that appeared under each photo identifying the location where Savanna snapped them. For the next few hours, Connor combed through Savanna's carefully staged and filtered photos until a pattern emerged. For the past several years, whenever Savanna stayed at a hotel, it was at one of the same two chains, Mendelson Hotels and Hospitality Inn. Since she was a Trans Air flight attendant, those must be the hotels the airline contracted with.

If Trans Air's hotel contracts were anything like other cooperate contracts, they were only good for a few years. Then the airline would re-evaluate the contract and either renew it or look for another hotel to partner with for the next few years.

Connor stood up from this chair with an aching head and strained eyeballs. Thanks to the postcard postmarks, Connor knew the sender was in Catasauqua, Pennsylvania, West Yellowstone, Montana, and Duluth, Minnesota, on June 7th the last three years.

And now he knew if the sender had stayed overnight in those cities, he had stayed at either Mendelson Hotels or Hospitality Inn, the airline's hotel partners. Connor had two pieces of the puzzle. He knew where the sender was and when he was there. Now he needed to know who he was.

11

SMILE AND DIAL

GETTING hotel records would be easier than getting flight manifest records directly from the airline, but it would still take some creativity.

Connor had a plan in his mind, and he hoped the Mendelson Hotels and the Hospitality Inn would play along. When looking for information, complicated schemes rarely work. Con jobs with multiple layers of deception are great for selling movie tickets, but in the real world, the more complicated something is, the more likely it is to fail.

US Army Intelligence had an extensive social engineering program, and Connor knew every page of the playbook. He'd learned various ways to psychologically manipulate someone into divulging confidential information without their knowledge of doing so. It was an ideal way to get people to talk without breaking fingers, waterboarding or otherwise violating the Geneva Convention.

The information Connor needed was inside the computers at Mendelson Hotels and Hospitality Inn, and he was going to get it without leaving Tara's office. Obtaining the hotels' guest information relied on one thing: plausibility. The quality of seeming reasonable. What were reasonable grounds a hotel employee would divulge who stayed at their hotel? That's private information, after all. The trick was to shift the motivation. Change the direction of the conversation from the hotel protecting its guest information to the manager wanting to shout it from the rooftops. That shift came down to incentive. That incentive would come in terms of money, or more specifically, the renewal of the lucrative Trans Air hotel contract.

Connor opened up a spoofing tool to create an email address. A quick search revealed Trans Air used the appropriately named @transair.com email extension. There was no way to create an account with that extension since it already existed, but he could create a similar one. He thought for a moment and then generated a legitimate-looking email account: roger_mathers@transairbenefits.com. It looked corporate enough, and since Connor, or Roger Mathers, was going to be calling from the benefits department, he thought it would pass muster. A few more stops on the information superhighway revealed Trans Air was based in Dallas, Texas. Dallas had a 214 area code. Connor opened another app on his phone to generate a Dallas phone number in case the hotel managers paid attention to those things. The secret to a solid con job was to remove all barriers of unbelievability. Never give a mark a reason to not believe.

The next step was to get the hotel manager on the phone. He looked up the number to the Mendelson Hotels property in Catasauqua, Pennsylvania, and dialed. A cheery woman named Ashley answered the line. Connor asked to speak with the manager, and after a brief hold, he found himself speaking to Christine Grote. He could hear her smile through the phone.

"Christine, this is Roger Mathers with Trans Air. I'm hoping you can help me with a delicate matter."

"I'll do my best. How can I help?"

"We've learned that one of our flight attendants has been misusing her hotel benefits. Letting friends stay for free on her account."

"That happens all the time," said Christine, still wearing the smile. "We tell our staff to check for airline IDs, but sometimes they forget."

"Totally understandable. I'm hoping you can pull a specific date range for me. I'm looking for the week of June 5th." Connor was most interested in any hotel stays around the 7th, but tossing out a week instead of a specific date seemed more realistic for someone trying to sniff out fraud.

"What's her name?" asked Christine.

Connor made up a name on the spot. It didn't matter what name he gave her because it wouldn't be in the hotel computer. That wasn't the point.

"Mandy Neely," he said. "She also goes by Amanda."

Christine typed away.

"I don't have anyone staying here that week by that name."

"I thought that might be the case," said Connor, sounding disappointed. "I've checked with other hotels, and her friends are using aliases. What about Cathy Allen or Deidre Haberstroh? Those were names they used at other hotels."

"Spell that last one for me."

"H-a-b-e-r-s-t-r-o-h."

"Nothing," she said. "Why don't I just send you the log

from that week, and you can cross-reference it with your manifest."

"That would be great."

Connor had hoped Christine would volunteer to send the log. He didn't want to ask for it, but that was the next play. The reason for the call was to get that list. He assumed Christine wanted to help Trans Air, and her hotel, crack down on fraud. Everyone in the hospitality industry wants to be helpful, and Christine didn't disappoint.

Connor gave Christine the Trans Air Benefits email address and joked about having a long list of hotels to call and not wanting to play benefits detective. She laughed and commiserated before hanging up the phone.

One down.

Connor took a deep breath and pulled up the number for the Mendelson Hotel in West Yellowstone, Montana. He duplicated the script, but this time, to cover his bases, he was looking for a pilot and not a flight attendant. He also asked for the records for the previous year and complained about how tough it was to investigate a series of fraudulent hotel stays from years back. The call flowed the same as the last, and by the time he hung up, the manager, John Ross, had committed to sending Connor the Trans Air hotel log for the weeks he needed.

His mobile phone chimed as he disconnected the call. It was Christine's email. He opened it to find a list of Trans Air employees who had stayed at the hotel the week in question. Six crew members stayed at the Mendelson Hotels property in Catasauqua on June 7th of this year. Now he had to wait for John's list and compare the two, hoping to find a common name. Connor waited for a half-hour, clicking refresh on his email program every few minutes. He was beginning to think the manager wasn't going to play along when a welcomed ding finally announced the email's arrival.

Connor compared the list from the two Mendelson Hotels for consecutive June 7^{ths} but there was no match. He slammed a heavy fist onto the desk, forgetting for a moment that it wasn't his.

There had to be a match. He compared the lists again in case he'd missed something, but there were no commonalities. Everything he planned to do next required a set of matching names.

He took a break and strolled down to Tara's boathouse to clear his head. Peering out over the water, he watched two fishing boats off in the distance. It was nearing three o'clock and the fish wouldn't be biting because of the heat. But sometimes being out on the water in a fishing boat not catching anything was still better than the alternative.

Connor kicked open one of Tara's dock chairs and watched the fishermen as he thought through his next steps. He wanted to have a common name to take to the Hospitality Inn. The plan was to find a match from the Mendelson Hotels Trans Air logs to confirm with the Hospitality Inn in Duluth, Minnesota. Any name that appeared on all three logbooks would be hard to discount. What were the odds of the same person being in the same cities where the last three postcards had been mailed?

He'd hoped to have more to go on, but decided to forge forward with a call to the Hospitality Inn anyway. There was still a chance that whoever was sending the postcards, if they did work for Trans Air, was not staying overnight. They could have flown in, mailed the card, and then took off again without a hotel stay.

Then it hit him. Connor only looked at June 7th, but what if they had flown in on June 6th, stayed at the hotel, and then mailed the card on the 7th before flying out again? He went back up to the house and checked the names from June 6th. There was one commonality: Jessica Winslow.

He called the Hospitality Inn in Duluth and ran through his spiel, but this time, he specifically asked the manager to look up Jessica for June 6th or 7th. The manager questioned why he was interested in an overnight stay from three years ago, but Connor diffused his skepticism by explaining they were going back several years looking for hotel stays that didn't match up to her flight schedule, which indicated someone other than Jessica used her name to book a free night at the hotel. He went on to explain that he had a spreadsheet full of dates where hotel stays were billed to the airline but where Jessica wasn't in that city. He felt his own blood pressure rising as he declared he'd make sure Jessica paid the airline back for every fraudulent stay and how he'd make sure she never worked for another airline. Connor almost believed it himself.

The ruse was still solid, and the manager confirmed that Jessica, or someone using her name, had checked in as an airline employee on June 6th, three years ago. Connor thanked the manager and hung up. No hotel log needed this time.

A quick search on a social media platform yielded three Jessica Winslows, but only one was a forty-eight-year-old flight attendant for Trans Air. He enlarged her profile photo and printed it out. Was he looking at the woman responsible for the murder of Little Freddie's wife and daughter? She didn't look like a murderer, and if she was a contract killer, why was she also working as a flight attendant? Traveling gave her access to cities across the country, but try as he might, Connor couldn't see this woman jetting across the states offing people in her spare time. It didn't add up, but he also couldn't shake the coincidence that she was in the same cities on the same days those postcards were mailed.

He opened another browser tab and pulled up another social media site, this one focused on careers and networking. He typed in Jessica's name and found that she had been a flight attendant for Trans Air for fifteen years. That fit Little Freddie's postcard timeline.

He went back to the other site and scrolled through her profile. He thought locating her would be more difficult, but her social media profile page indicated she lived in Tampa, Florida. He scoured through her timeline photos, which were all geotagged from different cities. He turned a page in his notebook and drew a line down the center. On one side, he listed all of the cities where Jessica had snapped photos. On the opposite side, he wrote the date the photo was taken.

It didn't take long for him to piece together her flight schedule based on when and where she took the photos. He knew she was in the air Monday through Wednesday, had Thursday off, was back in the air Friday and Saturday, and was off on Sunday.

Connor specialized in thorny jobs, solving unsolvable problems and finding people who didn't want to be found. When someone was underground, he had to get creative to locate them. But once he identified Jessica's name, he didn't have to work hard to find her. She advertised it for the world to see on social media. Connor had gone as far as he could go online. Now it was time to visit Jessica Winslow in person. If he was going to intercept her, he couldn't do it at an airport. Too much security. He'd have to do it at her home.

He went back to her social media feed. She had posted several photos with her daughter, who also lived in Tampa. He continued through the photo feed but found no pictures of a spouse, boyfriend, or girlfriend, which meant she likely lived alone. It wasn't a sure bet, but he'd confirm that when he got to her house. Connor made it a habit to always know what he was walking into.

He closed his notebook and cleared the history from Tara's Internet browser. Then he called an airline and booked a flight to Tampa for the following day.

12

SHE SELLS SANCTUARY

BOONE TURNED off Route 9 in Bangor and listened as the woman inside his cell phone directed him down several side streets until he rolled to a stop in the parking lot of the Bedford Lumber Company.

Stepping out of the vehicle, he looked at the front door. It was a refurbished barn door, the kind that slides on wrought-iron runners. It wasn't the door that caught his attention; it was the two video cameras positioned above it. Heavy security for a lumber company. He walked past a dark brown sedan parked next to a white pickup truck. The pickup was overflowing with parts, but they weren't anything Boone recognized. Not automotive parts, maybe industrial machinery. A quick check of the sedan's license plate confirmed he was in the right place.

He walked to the door and tried to push it open, but it was locked. He knocked. Then he knocked again. He kept at it until, finally, a latch disengaged on the other side and the heavy door rolled open.

"Whatcha need, fella?" The man asking the question

wore a tight-fitting white T-shirt that showed off his upper arms. He had slicked-backed hair and could have passed for a greaser from the fifties.

"You sell lumber, right?" said Boone. "I'll take some of that."

"Sorry, can't help you. Go somewhere else."

The door started to slide closed, but Boone stopped it with a size twelve black wingtip.

"This is a lumber company, right?"

"Yeah, it is. But we're closed."

"What's your name?"

"Collins."

"I need to have a word with you, Collins."

"I think you're in the wrong place, mister. You best turn 'round and go back to wherever you came from." He tried to close the barn door again, but Boone grabbed it and jerked it open, almost pulling Collins out of this T-shirt.

Collins reached for something behind him, but Boone already had a 9mm in his face.

"Inside." He motioned him in with the pistol.

"Buddy, I don't know who you are, but it's not smart to be waving that around here."

"Inside."

Boone followed Collins into the main room. The place had been a lumber operation at some point, but the saws had gone silent a long time ago. Now, the equipment wore more rust than sawdust. As they walked further into the building, he heard a radio playing from some distant room. He couldn't place the song. Maybe something by John Mellencamp.

"Your friend with the tattoo, where is he?"

"I don't know who you're talking about," said Collins.

"I don't ask twice," said Boone, raising the 9mm.

"Downstairs."

"Get him up here."

He followed Collins to the top of a stairwell. "Rockwell, I need you up here."

A minute later, a large man came up the stairs carrying a red duffle bag. He stopped when he saw the 9mm. "Who the fuck are you?"

Boone glanced down at the man's Semper Fi tattoo on his forearm. "The more pertinent question is who the fuck are you?" He motioned them to a plaid couch against the far wall.

Sitting down, the two men looked up at him.

"You two paid a friend of mine a visit. Connor Harding. I want to know who sent you and why." He leveled the weapon at Collins. "You first."

Collins was silent.

Boone pulled the trigger. The blast snapped Collins's head backward, cracking the glass window behind it.

"Your turn. I don't ask twice."

"Round Jon sent us," said Rockwell.

"Round Jon?"

"Yeah." The man shook on the plaid cushion.

"Why?"

"Albert Harding. Albert owes Round Jon for a ten-grand casino marker. He skipped town, and Round Jon sent us to see if he was in Meddybemps."

"Why did you fuck with Connor?"

"Albert wasn't there, but we heard his kid was staying on

the island. Round Jon said to knock him around a bit. To send a message to Albert. Get him to pay up."

"And you shot up his boat?"

"To send a message."

"You sent a message, all right."

"So, who are you?" asked Rockwell.

"Nobody." He fired two rounds into Rockwell's chest and headed toward the door. When he passed the room with the radio, it was playing "She Sells Sanctuary" by The Cult. That one, he recognized.

Back in the Mercedes, Boone scanned the scrap of paper Connor had given him and dialed. A moment later, Mitch Skinner answered.

"I need to get a message to Connor Harding."

"Okay," said Mitch.

"Tell him the license plate checked out, and it's not related to his case."

"Anything else?"

"His father owes someone named Round Jon ten grand."

"That fat ass?"

"You know him?"

"Yeah, he runs a small operation in Bangor," said Mitch.

"Well, the operation just got smaller."

13

JESSICA WINSLOW

THE EARLIEST CONNOR could get into Tampa was on flight 1053, which departed Bangor at nine a.m. It was a two-hour drive to Bangor from Meddybemps, which meant he had to leave the lake around five in the morning. Maine mornings were crisp, and when he stepped out of the cabin, the cold hit him like a fireplace poker to the jaw. Fog had settled over the lake, creating an eerie gray glow. Connor tossed his backpack and his Army duffle into the Boston Whaler, zipped his jacket up to his neck, and climbed aboard. The boat engine roared as he pulled away from the island and headed toward Mitch's dock. He stole a few glances back at the island, unsure if he'd return this summer. He hated the idea of cutting his vacation short, but there was only so much he could do sitting at Tara's PC. Eventually, he had to get into the thick of it.

Mitch's house was dark when Connor arrived at the dock. He tied off the boat and slipped the keys into the rusty mailbox bolted to the house next to Mitch's front door. Then he tossed his bags into the Jeep and rolled down the narrow driveway, his headlights slicing through the murky fog.

Connor used the two-hour wait at Bangor International to plan his encounter with Jessica. He used an online address database to locate her mailing address. All he needed was her name and state. Almost too easy.

Four Jessica Winslows appeared in the search results, but only one lived near Tampa. There was a unit number on the address, so Jessica lived in an apartment or condo. That made sense for a flight attendant who spent so much time away from home. He typed the address into a map website and was able to see a satellite view of her neighborhood. The image confirmed the place was an apartment complex. There was a parking lot in front of the building. He'd wait there for Jessica to come home, but he wasn't sure yet how he'd gain access to the unit.

He was thinking about that when his phone buzzed. He grabbed the phone in his left pocket, the one Little Freddie had given him, but it was silent. It was his personal phone.

"I was about to head over to the island when I saw the Whaler," said Mitch. "You in town?"

"Heading to Tampa."

"Why the hell would you do that?"

"Following a lead. What do you need, Mitch?"

"That big fella called me. Said to tell you the plate checked out and that your pops owes Round Jon quite a bit of money."

"That's why they sunk my boat?"

"Reckon so."

"Should I be worried?"

"I didn't take Round Jon as the violent type, but guess getting stiffed on ten grand will make anyone a bit mad."

"Jesus Christ. So we should expect a return visit?"

"Well, I got the impression your friend maybe stirred the pot a little bit. Assume Round Jon is going to be madder than he was yesterday."

"What did he do?"

"Didn't say, but I don't think it's good."

"I don't have time to worry about that right now. If you talk to my dad, let him know to watch his back when he comes back to Maine. And maybe check in on the island while I'm gone. Just in case he sends some else."

"Will do. You be careful in Florida."

"No promises."

Six hours later, Connor sat behind the wheel of a rental car on his way to Jessica Winslow's apartment complex. She lived fifteen minutes from the airport, and he arrived quicker than he thought he would.

The three-story complex included two buildings with twelve units each, six on the left and six on the right. A cluster of mailboxes stood next to a breezeway, which had concrete steps and thick wooded railings. Connor liked that each apartment had its own entrance. He wouldn't have to get through a centrally locked door and then into her apartment. But he didn't like that the breezeway was so open. Anyone could see him.

He stepped out of his rental and approached the mailboxes. Jessica's first and last name was on the box for unit three. It wasn't a complete confirmation, but the lack of a second name or "The Winslows" on the box hinted she lived alone. That's what he preferred. He didn't want an audience when he talked to her. Glancing up at the building, he noticed motion-activated floodlights on the corners but no security cameras.

Her unit was on the second floor of the breezeway at the front of the building. He could see her front door clearly from the parking lot, which meant everyone else could too. Connor could pick most locks in less than thirty seconds, but his tools were back in his Boston home. Even if he did have them, half a minute crouched in front of a doorknob could draw a lot of suspicion. A swift kick just to the side of the deadbolt would likely do the trick, but that option would be too loud, given the other units were so close. He'd have to find a quieter way.

Little Freddie's phone rang.

"What do you got?" he asked.

"Harding's boat issue wasn't connected to the postcards."

"You're sure?"

"Positive. Something about a gambling debt. His father's."

"They going to be a problem?"

"I took care of it."

"Good."

"There's something else. Harding's phone is in Tampa, Florida."

"Tampa?" said Freddie. "It must be something solid if he left Maine."

"That's what I thought."

"You better get down there. Retrace his steps and see what he knows."

After two hours baking in his rental, Connor watched a black Volkswagen Beetle roll into the lot and park in the spot with a large yellow three painted on the asphalt. A woman in a white button-up shirt and navy-blue skirt stepped out of the car and collected a rolling suitcase from the trunk. He got out of the rental as she headed for the breezeway stairs. He moved quickly, staying on the balls of his feet.

He had to time it just right. He didn't want to be right behind her when she slipped the key in the lock, but he needed to be close enough to get to her before she closed the door. He lagged behind her, and she was so wrapped up in getting her suitcase up the steps that she didn't notice him.

Connor listened for the deadbolt, and as soon she unlocked the door, he bounded up the stairs, taking them three at a time, and made it to her door just as she was wheeling the suitcase inside the apartment. He pushed her through the open doorway, kicking the door closed behind him. It took her a moment to realize what was happening, and in the confusion, Connor had already wrapped his forearm around her mouth, muffling any scream. He leaned into her, forcing her against the hallway closet door. He waited for her to stop struggling before he spoke.

"This may be hard to believe, but I'm not here to hurt

you. I just need some information, then I'll leave you alone. Do you understand?"

She nodded her head against his arm.

"Is there anyone else in the apartment?"

She motioned there was not.

"I'm taking my arm away. If you scream, bad things are going to happen."

The threat of violence was a powerful motivator, even if Connor had no intention of hurting her. He slowly removed his arm and waited to see how she would react. She didn't scream.

Connor motioned to the sofa in the living room. "Have a seat."

"What do you want?"

"I just want some information."

"People don't break into apartments for information. You're going to assault me. Or rob me."

"I'm not going to do either of those things. I just want to know why you're mailing postcards from all over the country."

She looked up at him, and the fear in her eyes seemed to turn to relief. She stepped back and sat on the sofa.

"How do you know about that?"

"So, you are sending them?"

She hesitated for a moment before nodding her head. "Who else knows it was me?"

It was a peculiar question.

"No one," said Connor.

"Why do you want to know about them?"

"Because the person you're sending them to hired me to find you."

84

Jessica Winslow was a tiny woman, maybe one-twenty-five soaking wet. She hadn't fought back when Connor entered the apartment. Nothing about her suggested she was violent.

"You don't look like a killer," said Connor.

She looked surprised. "I'm not a killer."

"My client believes whoever is sending the postcards killed his wife and daughter."

"I didn't kill anyone."

"There are details in the cards that only the killer would know."

"I've never read the postcards."

"What are you talking about? Of course you—"

"No. I'm only mailing them. He told me to mail them. Because I'm a flight attendant, I can mail them from different cities. I didn't write them."

"Who gave them to you?"

She hesitated.

"Jessica, who gave them to you?"

"He'll kill me."

"Who?"

She looked around the room and started to get up, but Connor pushed her back onto the sofa.

"Who?" he asked again.

She shook her head. "He'll kill my daughter."

"Listen very carefully," said Connor. "The man who hired me is a very dangerous person. He believes whoever is sending the postcards killed his family."

"I didn't kill anyone," she said.

"I believe you."

"Then you need to tell your friend that I had nothing to do with it."

"If you didn't have anything to do with it, why are you mailing the postcards?"

"Because if I don't, he'll kill Stephanie. He said so."

She wasn't budging, but Connor needed more information. He wasn't about to physically force it out of her, but there were other ways.

"Listen, Jessica. My client won't care much about the messenger. He just wants the man who pulled the trigger. I have to give my client a name, and I'd rather not give him yours."

She was shaking now.

Connor looked around the room. There was a television across from the sofa and a small computer stand with a PC in the corner. In the opposite corner was a small table with four framed photos, all of Jessica and someone Connor suspected was her daughter.

"Tell me who is forcing you to mail the postcards, and I can protect you. I can protect your daughter too. Once I give my client his name, he won't be around long enough to hurt anyone."

Jessica looked up at him. "I don't know his name."

"Then who is he?"

"I don't know. He contacted me by phone one day. Out of the blue. He knew I worked for an airline. He threatened me and Stephanie."

"Your daughter?"

Jessica nodded. "He said I had to mail something for him. He told me to go to a storage locker and get it. He said he'd hurt us, so I said I would. I thought it was drugs or something, but when I went to the locker, it was just an envelope. I thought it couldn't be something illegal, so I did it. I never heard from him afterward, so I thought it was a one-time thing. But then he contacted me again a year later telling me to do the same thing."

"And you mailed them every year?"

"Every year," she said.

"Did you ever go to the police?"

"And risk my daughter?" She shook her head. "Of course not."

"How does it work now? He still contacts you by phone?"

"A few times, he's slipped a note under my door. Just to prove he knows where I live. Once, he left me photos of two people he killed and said my daughter and I would end up the same way if I didn't cooperate."

"And you've never seen him? Never got a name?"

"No."

"Did he give you instructions with the envelope?"

"There is a postcard inside. I have to mail it at the airport. I just drop it in the box. I can't read the postcard and I have to mail it from whatever city I'm in on June 7th. That's it. That's all he told me."

"And you never look at it?"

"No. I don't want to know anything about it."

"Do you have any way to get ahold of him?"

"No."

"How did he find you in the first place?"

"I don't know. He knew I worked for an airline and that I had a daughter. He mentioned Stephanie by name, so I don't know if he knew her or not."

"Did you ask your daughter about him?"

She looked shocked at the question. "No. I didn't want to bring her into this." She wiped her sleeve across her eyes. The tears seeped through her silk sleeve. "I didn't want her to know about any of this."

"And you don't have any way to reach him. Any email or text?"

"No."

Either Jessica Winslow was telling the truth, or she was an impressive liar. Connor was convinced she didn't know who was giving her the postcards, but he also couldn't shake the thought the daughter was somehow connected. Maybe not directly, but she may be able to provide additional information. Jessica wasn't going to want to involve her, so Connor would have to push the right button.

"Where can I find your daughter?"

She shook her head. "I'm not going to tell you that."

"Jessica. I'm going to be straight with you. Your postcard friend, eventually, he's going to finish playing his little game with my client. And when he decides to pull the plug, what do you think he's going to do to you? Or Stephanie? He's already killed my client's family, and you said yourself he left you an example of his handiwork. Do you think he's going to just walk away? He won't think twice about killing you. And Stephanie. Help me find him, and I can stop all this."

She thought for a moment. "Are you going to break her door down too?"

"No. Tell me where I can find her, and I'll keep it nice and civil."

"Why should I trust you?"

"You can trust me because we both want the same thing —for all this to stop. I promise you, once I get his name, this all goes away. You and Stephanie won't be in any danger."

She was quiet for what seemed like two minutes, but Connor continued to stare her down. It was a tactic he learned in Army Intelligence. Remain quiet, and the person on the other side of the interrogation table will want to fill the silence. It was a way to keep someone talking. Eventually, they would tell you what you wanted to hear.

Finally, she looked up at Conner.

"You're not going to hurt her?"

"I'm here for the man behind the postcards. That's all."

She thought for a moment longer.

"She runs a bakery on Davis Island."

14

A FAMILIAR VOICE

THERE WAS one bakery on Davis Island. Cups and Cakes. It sold overpriced sweets to the kind of people who paid thirty-five dollars for a dozen cupcakes. There were two people in line when Connor arrived around four-thirty in the afternoon. The sign on the door said the place closed at five.

As Connor approached the counter, he observed the woman on the other side of the cash register. She looked to be in her early-to-mid-twenties. Flour covered her pink apron but spared her shoulder-length brown hair. The white embroidery on the front of her apron gave her away. Stephanie.

"What can I get for you?" she asked.

"Do you have root beer?"

"We don't have any soda."

"Coffee?"

"Of course."

"I'll take one of those."

She charged him three-fifty for a cup, spare change for the residents of Davis Island.

Connor paid with a crinkled five-dollar bill.

"Thanks." He took the steaming cup and change and pointed to a table along the wall. "I'm going to sit over there and drink this." He took a business card from the plastic tray on the counter. "Come see me when you close."

She forced a smile. "I have a boyfriend."

"Good for you, but I'm not looking for a date. I'm here to help your mother out of a very bad situation."

As Connor sat at the small corner table, Stephanie stole glances at him between closing duties. She cleaned behind the counter and restocked the bakery case. She took her time. He made her nervous, but she hadn't called the police yet, so she must be at least somewhat interested in what he had to say. She did disappear into the back room for ten minutes here and there, and Connor wondered if she had called her mother. Why wouldn't she? She'd want to know why he was there and how she was involved. Or maybe Jessica had called her before Connor even got there. She'd want to warn her, give her a heads-up of what was coming.

Forty-five minutes after he sat down, Stephanie approached the table.

"What's this all about?" she asked. "What are you talking about, helping my mother? And who are you?"

"Connor Harding. Your mother is being blackmailed into sending threatening postcards to a very bad man."

"She never mentioned anything about that to me. And I think she would have told me."

"There's a solid chance that whoever is blackmailing your mother also killed my client's wife and daughter."

"What does that have to do with me?"

"Whoever is blackmailing your mother is using you for leverage. He told her he'd kill you if she didn't do what he wanted. That's why your mother has been sending these postcards for the past decade."

"Decade?"

"Right. And the fact he's using you as leverage makes me think he knows you. And maybe you know him. He's close enough to your family to know you by name and know your mother's connection to the airline."

"Wait. Why does someone want my mother to send post-cards?" She pulled out the chair across from Connor and sat down. "That doesn't make any sense."

"Someone killed my client's family. Every year on the anniversary of their death, he receives a postcard. Taunts, grim details, that sort of thing. He's convinced whoever is sending them is responsible for the murders. Given the intimate details in there, I think he's right."

"And my mother is sending them?"

"Yes, but I don't think she's involved in the murders. Someone is giving her the postcards to send from all over the country to hide their whereabouts."

"But she doesn't know who?"

"No, but I don't think it's a random connection. They targeted your mother because she had the means to travel. And because they could also threaten you. That's why I think he's an acquaintance. He's got some familiarity with the two of you."

She thought for a moment. "Did my mom give you a description of the guy? That might help me narrow it down."

"They never met face-to-face. He used a drop to get her the postcards. That supports my theory that whoever is behind it knows your mother. He can't meet her in person because she'd recognize him."

Stephanie thought for a moment longer. "I can only think of one person."

"Who?"

"His name is Justin." She squinted her eyes. "Freeman?"

"Justin—"

"No, Friedman. Justin Friedman."

"Who is he?"

"My mother dated him for a little while. Years ago. It didn't last long. He was a dirtbag. I remember the police coming to our house looking for him a few times. He didn't live with us, but he was there a lot."

"Is she still in touch with him?"

"I doubt it. He was a mess. At one point, she had to get a restraining order against him. I know he was arrested at least once when they dated, but I don't remember why. I thought it was drugs, but I'm not positive. It was a long time ago. I do remember him stealing my mother's checkbook and draining her account. She couldn't prove it, though. Never got the money back."

"She never mentioned him when I spoke with her."

Stephanie shrugged her shoulders. "He's the only person I can think of." She shook her head. "I don't know if he could kill someone, but I wouldn't be surprised."

"Do you know where I can find him?"

"I have no idea. I don't even know if he's still in Florida. Probably in prison somewhere."

"He about your mother's age?"

"Yeah."

"White, black?"

"White."

"Can you think of anyone else?"

She glanced down and then around the room. Connor followed her eyes until they met his. "No. I can't think of anyone else who would do something like this and that has a connection to our family."

Connor wrote down his cell number on the back of the business card he took from the counter. "If you think of someone else, call me. This is very important, Stephanie. There's a lot of evil people wrapped up in this, and it's best if we all get out as quickly as possible."

She nodded as he stood up and headed for the door.

"What's going to happen to him? To Justin?" she asked.

The question caught Connor off guard. It showed sympathy, as if she was worried about him.

"Nothing good."

Back at his rental car, Connor slipped out his phone, and after spending a few minutes looking up North Carolina law offices, he dialed.

After talking his way through an operator and an administrative assistant, he got Tara Savage on the line.

"Didn't think I'd ever hear from you," she said.

"I'm not that kind of guy."

"How's Maine?"

"It was fine when I left yesterday. I'm in Tampa now."

"Tampa? For that case you're working on?"

"Right. I need a favor. I'm hoping you can help."

"A favor? Are we at that stage in our relationship?"

"I think so," said Connor. "Doesn't that come right after attempted murder on a watercraft?"

He waited for a laugh, but it didn't come.

"What's the favor?"

"You said you've got a few PIs working for you. I could use some help locating someone. Figured they could do it a lot faster than me."

She was quiet, and Connor thought she was thinking of an excuse to stay out of this.

"What's the name?" she asked.

"Justin Friedman." He spelled out the last name. "Caucasian. In his late forties or early fifties. Tampa, Florida, was his last known place of residence."

"That's all you got?"

"That's it," he said.

"I'll see what our guys can dig up."

"You think you can get it to me today?"

"Today?" she snapped.

"It's really important. And I'll make it up to you."

"Oh, you'll make it up to me. I'll see what they can do."

"I appreciate it, Tara."

"I know you do. It's good to hear your voice again, Connor. I had a bad feeling that something had happened to you."

"Not yet."

"If your work ever brings you to Charlotte, look me up."

"I'll do that," said Connor.

"And be careful in Florida."

"No promises."

15

FINDING JUSTIN FRIEDMAN

CONNOR CHECKED into a hotel a few miles from Stephanie's bakery. Justin Friedman was his best lead, but he had no idea where to find him. He hoped Tara's private investigator could throw him a bone. He also hoped Justin was still in Florida. He preferred to stay close in case he had to go back to Jessica or Stephanie for more information.

He was at the hotel restaurant eating lobster ravioli when his cell vibrated on the white tablecloth. It was Tara.

"You got something for me?"

"We're already dismissing the pleasantries?" she asked.

"I figure neither of us is the type to waste time."

"Your man is still in Florida. His address is sixty-one-ten Black Marlin Lane in Cape Coral."

"Thank you. That's extremely helpful."

"My PI also ran his record, and it's pretty colorful. Popped a few times for petty theft and check fraud. Did six months for assault. They also got him for selling narcotics, but they dropped the charges. He probably rolled on someone. Seems like a real winner. You should introduce him to your father. They'd probably get along swell."

"My father already hangs out with enough degenerates. I don't need to add any more to the mix."

"You going to go talk to this guy?"

"Reckon so."

"I'd be careful if I were you. He looks pretty dangerous."

"They always are."

He thanked her and hung up the phone just as the waitress brought the check.

A few minutes after ten p.m., a Cessna Citation CJ3 touched down on runway 10-28 at Tampa International. After it pulled into a private hanger, a man in a gray suit and black wingtips descended the steps and climbed into a waiting sedan.

The next morning, Connor grabbed the continental breakfast at the hotel. He opted for a Spanish omelet and a banana nut muffin. He wanted to go back for another omelet, but there was a line, so he refilled his coffee and pocketed a second muffin instead.

Justin Friedman lived 130 miles from Tampa. Connor had lucked out. Jessica's ex-boyfriend hadn't wandered too far over the years.

Connor followed the directions on his phone, and after two hours on the road, he arrived at the address. He looked up to find a sun-bleached sign for the Seaside Marina and

Resort. The place fit into the first category, but "resort" was a stretch. As he looked out over the marina, he counted three dozen boats, all in various states of disrepair. He figured only half of them were still seaworthy.

Marinas were synonymous with temporary living, and he hoped Justin was still there. Connor checked the information Tara sent for a slip number, but there wasn't one. After he parked the rental car, he grabbed his backpack and walked past a small coffee shop toward the main office. He'd ask the clerk if Justin was still renting a slip. If he wasn't, he'd ask for a forwarding address. If that fell through, Connor might be back to square one.

He decided to stay on the positive side and took a deep breath as he approached the office. The pungent scent of fish and boat gas hit him like smelling salts. He swallowed the smell and jerked on the office door handle. Had it not been for two rusty bolts that refused to give up, the handle would have snapped off.

Behind the office counter was an older man who looked like he'd rather be somewhere else. His deep tan suggested he spent more time outdoors than in.

Connor approached him and placed his hands on the counter. "Hoping you could help me."

"How's that?"

"I'm looking for one of your renters. Justin Friedman."

The man's eyes narrowed. "What do you want with that piece of shit?"

Connor patted his backpack. "I'm here to serve him papers. Can you tell me which slip he's in?"

"Figures. He's in sixteen."

"He been renting long?"

"About a year and a half. He owes two months back rent, so I'm not sure how much longer he'll be here. I gave him one extension, but there ain't gonna be a second."

"Do you know if he's there now?"

"No idea."

Connor looked out the window as the man stepped out from behind the counter and pointed.

"Sixteen is over there," he said. "It's the white and blue houseboat."

"Got it." Connor thanked him and left.

"Tell him to pay his dock rent, or I'll tow that piece of shit out of there!"

"Will do."

Slip sixteen was on the east side of the marina. There, moored to the dock was a thirty-foot single-deck houseboat. As houseboats go, it was on the small side. It was white with a faded blue stripe running down the side. Thanks to the drawn curtains and tinted windows, Connor couldn't tell if anyone was inside.

There were two other boats attached to the same dock as Justin's houseboat, a dilapidated yacht and a medium-sized houseboat. Connor looked for anyone who might see him skulking around, but the place was deserted. He stepped over the frayed rope railing onto the deck of Justin's houseboat. He passed the rusted barbecue grill and plastic deck chair and knocked on the sliding glass door. No answer. He knocked again. Justin wasn't there.

Connor checked over his shoulder, and when he was satisfied no one was watching him, he grabbed the door handle and pulled. The door opened without any argument. Inside, Connor walked through the living quarters. The bed was unmade and clothes littered the floor. In the kitchen, he opened the small refrigerator to find fresh milk and a few other essentials. Someone definitely lived here.

Papers littered a small table on the wall opposite the refrigerator. Connor dug through them and quickly found what he was looking for. Several bills addressed to Justin Friedman. It was in the right place, but was Justin the right guy? He scoured through the mess of papers on the table and found a grocery list.

Rummaging through his backpack, he removed a handful of postcards and set them down on the table next to the grocery list. The list didn't give him a lot to work with, but it was enough. He compared the shapes and curves of the handwriting. He examined the stroke direction, legibility, letter size, and whether the loops were rounded or angled. The handwriting on the grocery list and the postcards appeared to belong to the same person. It wasn't a scientific analysis, and it would never hold up in court, but it didn't have to. Justin Friedman was his guy. But where was he?

He'd have to wait to find out. It was only 10:30 a.m., and it could be hours, if not days, before Justin returned to the boat. There wasn't much here to come home to. Connor remembered the coffee shop he had passed on his way to the marina office and decided he'd keep an eye on the place from there. He slid the glass door closed behind him and stepped back onto the dock, looking again for anyone who may have seen him.

A few minutes later, he was standing at the counter inside the coffee shop. Below the counter next to the cash register was a six-inch knife littered with bagel crumbs. He ordered a coffee, and when the coffee jock turned around to pour it, he swiped the knife, tucked it into his back pocket, and covered it with his shirttail. By the time the woman returned with his coffee, his hands were slipping a five-dollar bill from his wallet.

He told her to keep the change, took the coffee, and headed for the front patio, which overlooked the marina. He carefully slipped the knife out of his pocket and slid it into his sock, covering it with his pants leg before sitting down. He sipped from the paper cup—the coffee was twice as good and half as cheap as Cups and Cakes—and surveyed the marina. From his cafe table, he had a clear view of Justin's slip.

An hour ticked by, but the only thing that caught Connor's attention was a group of older men fishing from a nearby dock. He was reaching down to reposition the knife in his sock when the woman who had served him the coffee appeared next to him.

"Refill?" she asked.

"Sure."

She filled his cup from the black carafe in her hand. "You waiting for someone?"

"Yeah, someone from the marina."

"I think they stood you up."

Connor reached for his cell phone and found the email Tara had sent him. He clicked on the attachment and opened Justin's booking photo.

"You ever see this guy?"

She studied it. "Don't think so. He lives at the marina?"

"That's right."

She shook her head. "Maybe he's come in. We get a lot of people from the marina, but I don't recognize him by the picture. I can ask my manager if you want."

"No, that's okay."

She looked him up and down. "You're not from around here, are you?"

"Why do you ask?"

"You're wearing long pants, a flannel shirt, and boots. And you don't look like a fisherman."

"I was in Maine twenty-four hours ago. It's colder there."

"You on vacation?"

"Business."

"With the guy in that picture?" she asked.

"Something like that."

After the woman left, Connor returned his eyes to slip sixteen.

He had just finished the second cup of coffee when he saw a man walking down the dock toward Justin's house-boat. Connor approached the railing to get a better look. As he stepped, the tip of the blade jabbed the side of his foot. His eyes followed the man, and he watched as he climbed aboard Justin's boat.

Connor retrieved the knife from his sock, returned it to his back pocket, and left the coffee shop for the dock. He approached slip sixteen to find the man dumping the gray coals from the grill over the side of the boat into the water. He stopped when he saw Connor.

"What the hell are you looking at?" he asked.

Connor studied his face and mentally compared it to the booking photo. It was Justin Friedman.

"Nothing," said Connor. "Just out for a stroll."

"Well, go stroll somewhere else, asshole."

Connor moved along to the end of the dock, turned around, and walked back toward the houseboat. Once he saw Justin slip inside the boat, Connor leaped onto the deck's edge and over the rope railing. He pulled the knife out of his back pocket, steadied his backpack, and slid the door open. Justin was holding a bag of charcoal.

"What the fuck?" Justin stared at Connor, confused, not sure what was happening. As Connor approached, Justin threw the bag at Connor, who stepped to the side. The bag slammed into the glass door, sending coals across the floor and a plume of black dust into the air.

"I got nothing for you to steal, man," he said, keeping his eyes on the knife and backing unto the kitchen.

"I'm not here to steal anything," said Connor. "Just want to ask you some questions."

"With a knife?" Justin turned and grabbed a pair of scissors from the kitchen table."

"Put those down." Connor returned the knife to his back pocket to reduce the threat level. "Just want to talk."

"Did Moody send you? Fuck him."

Justin lunged, the scissors raised. Connor grabbed his wrist with both hands, pulled down, and turned, locking his arm at the elbow and dragging him to the ground. He continued to twist, far enough to get Justin to drop the scissors but not far enough to dislocate his arm.

Once Connor had him on the ground, he drove his knee into Justin's ribs, cracking at least one, maybe two. Justin screamed, and Connor shoved his face into the torn carpet to muffle the sound while he kicked the sliding glass door closed.

"You done?" said Connor.

"What do you want?"

"I want to talk to you about Little Freddie."

"Who?"

"Freddie and your postcards."

"What postcards?"

Connor stood up and rolled him over. "Cut the shit. The postcards you're giving to Jessica Winslow."

"Jess? She sent you?" Justin slowly stood up, rubbing his shoulder. "This about those fucking checks? That was forever ago."

"This is about you blackmailing Jessica to send those postcards to Freddie."

"I don't know who that is." He rubbed his shoulder again and winced.

Connor studied his face. "You know Jessica?"

"Yeah, I know her."

"When was the last time you contacted her?"

"I don't know. Ten years, maybe?" Justin stared at Connor, his eyes wide.

The US Army had spent a lot of time and money teaching Connor how to spot a lie. It was a cornerstone of interrogation because information is useless if it isn't true. There were a variety of ways to spot a liar. The eyes, the mouth, even the hands. Subtle movements will betray anyone, but you had to know what to look for. And Connor knew what to look for.

"How do you know Jessica?"

"Used to see her. You know, on and off. Forever ago. When she first moved to Florida."

"How long were you together?" Connor kept following his eyes.

"Not long. A year maybe. Didn't work out."

"Why are you sending the postcards to my client?"

"I told you, I don't know anything about any postcards."

"Cut the bullshit." Connor slid his backpack off, unzipped it, and handed Justin the first postcard he grabbed. "I compared your handwriting from the grocery list on your table. You wrote them."

Justin stared at the card and then flipped it over a few times. He tried to string a thought together but was having a hard time.

"Wait," he said. "Did Jess give these to you?"

"She sent them to my client, Little Freddie. You gave them to her to send."

"No."

"It's your handwriting—"

"I know it is." He studied the card again and then sat down on the sofa to collect his thoughts. "I remember writing these, but that was forever ago."

"You gave her one of these just a month ago."

"No, I didn't. I haven't seen these in years."

Connor studied his body language. He had to be lying, but he appeared to be telling the truth. The handwriting matched. It had to be him.

"You're lying to me," he said.

"I'm not. I'm not mailing anything." He wiped his face. "And you still haven't told me who you are." He started to stand, but Connor's size twelve knocked him back onto the couch.

"Someone is sending my client postcards about his dead wife and daughter. And that someone is you."

"No, it's not."

"You're blackmailing Jessica to send them from across the country. You killed Little Freddie's wife and daughter and you've been taunting him ever since."

Justin studied the postcard again and shook his head. After a moment, he looked up at Connor with renewed focus in his eyes. "I remember now. I wrote them. I remember. But I didn't tell Jess to send them. And I sure as hell didn't kill anyone."

"You remember writing them?"

"Yeah. I do now." He handed the card back to Connor. "I wrote them for Jess."

"What?"

"But that was years ago. When we were still together."

"What are you talking about?" Connor kicked the side of Justin's shin. "Explain!"

"When I first started seeing Jessica, she had just come to Florida. With her kid." He wiped his face again. "They had only been here a few months. Told me she just got out of an abusive relationship. She never really talked about it, just that it was bad. That's why she came to Florida. To get away from him."

He seemed to be stalling.

"What does this have to do with the postcards?"

"Jess thought her ex might come looking for her. Her daughter too. She was scared of him. I remember that. Real scared of him."

Connor kicked him again. "The postcards?"

"She asked me to write out a whole bunch of these. She

said if her ex thought she was dead, he wouldn't come looking for her. She was going to send them to her ex-husband. She wanted me to write them because she said he'd recognize her handwriting. I didn't think she was serious about going through with it."

"She came to Florida to get out of a relationship?"

"Yeah."

"Where did she move from?"

"No idea. Forget, if I ever knew."

"She say anything else about the guy she was running from? Ever mention his name?"

"Maybe, I don't know. Look, that was a long time ago, and you forget things, you know?"

Connor thought back to Jessica. Little Freddie said his wife and daughter were murdered about twelve years ago, and he mentioned his daughter was about ten years old at the time. Connor did the math in his head.

The ages fit.

"Look, man," said Justin. "I didn't kill anyone, and I don't know who this Little Freddie guy is. I got nothing to do with whatever you're looking for."

Connor believed him. Justin Friedman may have played a minor role in all this, but he wasn't aware of it. And he didn't kill Little Freddie's wife and daughter. No one did.

They were alive and well. In Tampa.

16

NOT-SO-DEAD ENDS

Boone opened an app on his cell phone. His screen showed a history of locations where the cell phone in Connor's pocket had been, the digital breadcrumbs he had left behind. Now, he was parked at an apartment complex with two three-story brick buildings on Foxtail Lane. A blue thumbtack icon appeared over a satellite image of the complex on the phone's screen. He pinched the screen and zoomed in, and a digital blue thumbtack bobbed and flickered until it rested between the two buildings on the image.

"Shit."

Somewhere, up in space, a satellite had been able to track Connor's cell phone to the property, even placing him between these two buildings, but it wasn't precise enough to know the exact unit he had visited. Only the general area.

Boone scrolled through the other results on the app, clicking off the apartment complex and onto the next stop on Connor's trip. That location, a bakery on Davis Island, was much easier to pinpoint.

He tossed the phone aside, started the sedan, and pulled out of the parking lot.

Connor sat in his rental at the marina parking lot, watching two seagulls fight over a discarded bagel. Everything Justin said led Connor to believe Stephanie knew Little Freddie a lot more than she let on. The pieces were slowly falling into place, but the picture Justin painted didn't match the one Little Freddie described. According to Freddie, his wife and daughter were long dead, and he very well might think that was the case. But that storyline was crumbling.

Connor had to take a step back and reset his investigation. Before finding the person responsible for killing Freddie's family, he had to confirm if they were dead. His gut said no, but that had been wrong before. He pulled out his phone and looked up the nearest library. The Cape Coral Library was on Mohawk Parkway, only a few miles from the marina. He was there in ten minutes.

From the outside, the Cape Coral Library looked like an ornate Spanish mission. Its beige stucco walls and red ceramic roof tiles didn't give off the usual library vibes, and as public libraries go, Connor thought it was hands down the nicest one he'd ever seen. The inside was just as impressive. Wide archways separated side rooms from the main hallway. Bronze busts of famous authors lined the hallway, and the smooth, curved oak accents on the bookshelves were a stark contrast to the sharp metal edges of the library in Calais, Maine.

Connor followed the signs to the computer lab, confident there was no photograph of his father behind the counter.

After a quick conversation with the aide, Connor was sitting in front of a brand new laptop locked to the glossy, oak table by a thin cable.

He opened his notebook and went to work. Little Freddie said his wife and daughter were murdered twelve years ago. If that were true, the local Columbus, Ohio, media would have covered it from every angle. Murdered white women sold newspapers and airtime.

Connor navigated to the website for the *Columbus Dispatch* and headed to the archives. He ran a search for the murder of Debra Blasko, but nothing came up. He left the *Columbus Dispatch* site and expanded to a general Internet search but still found nothing. The news of a woman and her young daughter's murder should have been easy to find. It wasn't, and that was a problem.

Little Freddie's version of the story was collapsing. Could Little Freddie have kept it out of the media? The local police would have responded to the murder. Given Little Freddie was in the business of killing people and likely had powerful friends, he could have somehow suppressed it, but why? Media coverage could help flush the killer out. To people like Freddie, the murder of his family could be a sign of weakness. Someone got to him. That could be bad for business. Even though that scenario was unlikely, it was still a possibility.

To confirm Debra's death, Connor could contact the Ohio Department of Health's vital statistics department and order her death certificate. But that would take weeks, and that was time he didn't have.

He decided to dive deeper into Freddie's version of the

story. Connor picked up the phone Little Freddie had given him and dialed the only number in the contact list.

"You got an update for me?" said the gravelly voice on the other end.

"Working on an angle, but I need some info from you."

"What's that?"

"I want to see the case file for the murders. Did you ever get a copy, or can you get one through Columbus PD?"

Little Freddie was silent on the other end. It was a legitimate question, as that file could provide details to aid Connor's investigation.

"Freddie?" said Connor.

"There is no case file."

"As in you don't have it, or it doesn't exist?"

"It doesn't exist. There was no investigation."

"What do you mean there was no investigation? Why not?"

"I didn't report it."

"Who found the bodies? They would have called the police."

"No bodies."

Connor didn't say anything.

"There were no bodies, Connor."

"We need to back up then. You said they were killed returning from your daughter's dance class."

"They were."

"Excuse the stupid question, but if there were no bodies, how do you know they were murdered?"

"They didn't return that night, and the next day, someone left a package on my porch. It was my daughter's ballet slippers. They were covered in blood. Whoever killed them didn't leave the bodies, but they made sure I knew what happened. That's how these things work, Connor. They're probably buried in a cornfield somewhere in Indiana."

"You left that part out of our initial conversation."

"What difference does it make? It was a retribution killing. Bodies don't always turn up. You should know that."

Connor did know that. Three years ago, he was working for the New York mob. Criminals disappeared all the time. Sometimes their bodies turned up, and sometimes they didn't. Their families were usually off-limits, but the New York crime families played by an official set of rules. Whoever went after Little Freddie didn't have that playbook.

"The police report wouldn't have given you anything anyway," said Freddie. "Where are you?"

"I'm in Florida."

"You're onto something then?"

"Following up on a lead, but I don't have anything concrete yet. I'll call you as soon as I have something definite."

Connor hung up the phone before Freddie could respond.

Stephanie Winslow was refilling the bakery cabinet, carefully aligning a row of banana nut muffins, when the bakery door opened. A man in a gray suit stepped to the counter.

"What can I do for you?" asked Stephanie.

"It all looks so good. How do I decide?"

"We're known for our cupcakes. Blueberry is my favorite. I can heat it up for you. They're even better warm."

He bent over the counter, peering through the freshly cleaned glass. "You know, that sounds delicious."

He was crouched over, examining the contents of the cabinet, when Stephanie caught a glimpse of the inside of his suit jacket. There was a handgun holstered below his left armpit.

She collected a blueberry muffin and headed for the microwave.

"I'm also interested in talking to you about a man who came in here yesterday. About my height, stocky, short beard. Name's Connor Harding. I'd like to know what you two talked about."

Stephanie fumbled with the paper wrapping on the cupcake. "Hmm, I don't know anyone by that name. You sure he came here?"

"I'm positive he came in here." He tapped on the counter. "You work yesterday?"

"I did, but not all day."

"What shift did you work?"

"I came in around noon and stayed until I closed the place."

"Then you must have seen him. He was here at four-thirty-seven."

"That's pretty specific."

"Gotta love technology."

"Well, I don't remember him. I don't remember talking to anyone, aside from general chitchat." She walked to the microwave, placed the muffin inside and set the time. "Just a second on that muffin."

"You wouldn't lie to me, would you?"

"What do you mean?"

"The man who came in here. I really need to know what he discussed with you."

"I'm sorry, I can't help with that. As I said, I don't remember speaking with the person you described. We get a lot of customers, but it's just general hellos and whatnot." She looked around. "One sec, I need to grab more paper plates."

Stephanie stepped into the kitchen at the back of the bakery and opened the back door as quietly as she could. She began running just as the microwave's timer dinged.

Connor picked up his cell and dialed Tara. He didn't know how much she was willing to do for him, but he had another favor.

"Sick of me yet?"

"Getting there."

Connor could sense her smile through the phone. At least, he hoped it was a smile.

"I promise this will be the last time you hear from me."

"I hope not," she said.

"I mean in the favor capacity. I don't want you to think I'm taking advantage of you."

"You are taking advantage of me."

Connor didn't know how to respond.

"But I'm okay with that. I want to help. What's going on?"

Connor was about to ask Tara if her investigators could dig up anything on the Debra Blasko murder, but he decided to switch gears. "Can you have your boys look into a Jessica

Winslow?" He spelled the name. "Four-four-zero-eight Foxtail Lane. Apartment three. Tampa, Florida."

She repeated it back to him. "This your suspect?"

"One of them. And thank you."

"I'll see what they can come up with. And you're welcome."

He clicked off the phone. He needed to talk to Jessica again. He wanted to look into her eyes when he told her what Justin had said about her asking him to write the postcards. That confession put a sinkhole in her blackmail story. But he wanted more information on her before knocking on her apartment door.

He remembered from his notes that Jessica was flying today but should return sometime this evening. In the meantime, he'd use that time to revisit Stephanie. Connor was still unclear what Stephanie knew about what was going on. Had she been a part of the scheme the entire time? If so, she would have wanted to protect her mother, but why did she give him Justin's name. Why bring him into the mix and risk outing her mother as a liar? Jessica likely sent Connor to her daughter because she was confident Stephanie wouldn't give him anything useful. Maybe she had inadvertently.

Connor was flipping through his notebook when his cell rang.

"There's a man in the bakery asking about you," said Stephanie. "He has a gun."

"What?"

She repeated herself.

"Who is he?"

"Don't know. Tall, big guy in a suit."

"Shit."

"He knew you were here. He wanted to know what we talked about."

"What did you say?"

"Nothing."

"Where are you now?"

"I slipped out the back door and ran to a cafe. It's a quarter-mile from the bakery."

"Did he see you?"

"I don't think so."

"Is your mother still flying today?"

"Yeah, why?"

"If he knows I saw you, maybe he knows I saw her, too."

"I can call her," said Stephanie.

"Do that. Tell her not to go back to her apartment."

"Okay."

"I'll come get you. Is there any place you can stay that isn't home?"

"I have a rental property. I can stay there."

"Sit tight and don't leave the cafe. Send me the address, and I'll be there as soon as I can."

He hung up the phone and turned the wheel toward Tampa.

17

ALFRED

CONNOR SLOWLY ROLLED through the strip mall parking lot, scanning the area. The man Stephanie described matched Boone's description, but why was he in Tampa, and how did he know Connor was there? Connor had mentioned Florida when he spoke with Little Freddie hours earlier, but he must have already been here. Somehow, he had been tailing Connor, but for how long?

Picking up his cell phone, he clicked on Stephanie's number. She was on the line a moment later.

"I'm here," said Connor. "Have you seen the guy since the bakery?"

"No."

Connor looked up at the store marque and rolled to a stop in front of the cafe.

"I'm outside."

"Be right out."

Connor took another look around and opened the passenger door as Stephanie ran toward the car. She stopped at the open door and hesitated.

"How do I know I can trust you?" she asked.

"You need to get in before someone sees you."

"I don't even know who you are."

"We're on the same side here, Stephanie. The man who came into your bakery, his name is Boone. He's looking for your mother. I can explain later, but you need to get into the car now."

"Who is he?"

"Your father sent him."

Her eyes widened, and she took a step back. Connor thought she might run. "My father?"

"I'll explain everything, just get in."

Connor could see her curiosity tugging her toward the vehicle, like some strong gravitational pull. She hesitated again but finally slipped into the car. Connor hit the gas, checking his rearview for a tail. When he pulled out into traffic, he was certain no one was following them.

"Spill it," she said.

"First, where are we going?"

Stephanie gave him directions to her rental property on Indian Rocks Beach and they settled in for the ride.

"When did you first come to Florida?" asked Connor.

"We moved here when I was just a kid."

"What do you remember about your life before moving here?"

"Nothing worth talking about. We lived in Ohio for a while. We moved around a lot."

"What do you remember about your father?"

"I know he's dead."

"What else do you know about him?"

"My mother said he was mixed up with some bad people

who killed him. Drugs or something. We moved here to get away from all of it."

"And your mother, she changed her name? And yours?"

"To protect us, yes. She never wanted anyone connected with my father to find us. She said the people who killed him, that they might come looking for us." She looked over her shoulder out the rear window. "That's what this is all about? Is someone who knew my father coming for us?"

"Your father is still alive, Stephanie."

She looked at him. "No. He's been dead for years."

"That's what your mother told you, but he's not dead. She was right that he was associated with some bad people. Real bad people. She must have wanted a way out and brought you to Florida to get away from him."

"I don't believe you."

"Believe it. Your father hired me to find you. Well, kind of."

"What do you mean?" Stephanie looked over her shoulder again and slid down in the passenger seat.

"When your father hired me, he gave me a box of post-cards," said Connor. "He thought whoever was sending them killed you and your mother twelve years ago."

"But if we're not dead, who was sending them? And why?"

"Your mother sent them. She wanted to keep up the illusion that you two had been killed."

Stephanie was processing the last twelve years, second-guessing everything her mother had told her.

"Something's been bothering me about all this," continued Connor. "I have to believe your father thought you two were dead. Otherwise, he wouldn't have waited twelve years to come looking for you. I think something tipped him off and changed his mind, but I don't know what. I think he knew you and your mother were alive when he hired me. And he assumed I'd eventually stumble onto you."

"What about this Boone person?" she asked. "What does he have to do it?"

"Your father must have sent him after me. To tail me and see where the investigation took me."

"Why?"

"Because he knew if I figured it out and realized you and your mother were alive and in hiding that I'd never turn you over to him. He sent Boone down here to make sure that didn't happen."

"So he wants to kill us? His own family?"

"I'm not sure, but Little Freddie has been lying to me from the start, and that man who came to your bakery is really bad news. I need to get you and your mother someplace safe until I can figure this out."

"His name is Alfred."

"What?"

"You called him Little Freddie. His name is Alfred." Stephanie turned, rested her chin on the soft leather seatback, and stared out the rear window as they drove across the Howard Frankland Bridge toward Largo, Florida.

Stephanie's rental property was a small cottage on Indian Rocks Beach. White shiplap siding and blue trim covered the place. This part of the beach didn't have many homes, but a half-mile down, the coastline was littered with bungalows and hotels.

After entering the four-digit code on the front door deadbolt, they stepped inside. The cottage was small, not suited for full-time living, but perfect for a vacation getaway. It had a living area and kitchen in the main room and a small bedroom and bathroom off to the side. The entire place was in a state of renovation. There were tools and building materials scattered everywhere. On the floor sat unfinished pine boards for molding, beadboard for the walls, tubes of adhesive, several unopened paint cans, and a ladder that was on the wrong side of steady.

"You should be safe here," said Connor. "But stay inside." He looked at the refrigerator. "Do you have food here?"

"No, but there's a local grocery in town that delivers. Lots of restaurants too."

"Good. Then stay put for a while, and I'll check in after I find your mother." Connor checked his watch. "What time does she get in tonight?"

"A few hours."

"Sit tight. I'll call you when I talk to her." Connor headed for the door. "Lock this behind me."

Boone watched the front door of Cups and Cakes bakery from the parking lot. No sign of Stephanie. His eyes moved down to the cell phone in his hand. He examined Connor's route over the last several hours. The phone Little Freddie gave Connor started the day in Tampa and then headed south on I-75 to Cape Coral. He checked the time stamp on the

GPS app. The phone spent several hours at a marina in Cape Coral and then returned along the same route to Tampa.

He zoomed in again and followed the red line to a location not far from where he sat.

"So, that's where you went."

He rechecked the trip log to see the phone had traveled from that location to Indian Rocks Beach. According to the time stamp, he had only been there fifteen minutes and was now traveling on I-275 North.

"Why are you coming back here, Connor? Back to the apartment complex, maybe? Who's there?" Boone thought for a moment. "And why were you at the beach." He traced the red line with his fingers again. "You dropped her off."

He fired the engine and rolled out of the parking lot, following the app's route to Connor's last location on Indian Rocks Beach.

18

TAMPA INTERNATIONAL

THE SUN WAS SETTING when Connor arrived at Tampa International Airport. Jessica's return leg was due to land in the next forty-five minutes. He found a spot in the parking garage and walked into the terminal.

Connor had to intercept Jessica before she left the airport. Boone had found the bakery, and Connor assumed he had also found Jessica's apartment. He didn't want her going back there before he had a chance to talk to her. That meant meeting her at the gate when she arrived. To do that, he needed a ticket.

Connor despised airports. He hated throngs of people, and airports were usually packed wall to wall with people in a hurry but not exactly sure where they were going. Tonight was different, though. Tampa International was a bustling airport, but this time of night, things were calm. With only a few flights departing this late, the ticket counters were quiet and lightly staffed. Except for a lanky woman in a navy blue skirt and suit jacket with a tan scarf around her neck, the Trans Air ticketing area was desolate.

The ticket agent had a kind face and a corporate grin, but that didn't translate into conversation. That suited Connor just fine. The last thing he needed was a curious agent questioning his ticket purchase for a flight that same night or why he had no bags, both red flags in commercial aviation. A few minutes and nearly eight hundred dollars later, he pocketed the paper ticket and went to the bright overhead arrival/departure screen to locate Jessica's gate.

From his initial research back in Maine, he knew Jessica would be returning tonight from Memphis. He squinted at the flickering screen and found her arriving flight on the board. Gate C-7. He moved toward security as quickly as he could without drawing attention to himself. He wasn't surprised when he got pulled aside for a security pat down. The ticket agent had likely flagged him as a suspicious passenger. He'd expected that.

After ten minutes in the security line, he made his way through the terminal and joined the group of passengers waiting for their departing flight out of C-7. Before they could go anywhere, they'd need a plane, and that was still en route from Memphis. Connor split his time watching the wall clock and an unruly kid pummeling a computer tablet with his fist. The woman sitting next to the boy seemed content letting him test the effectiveness of the thick green rubber protector encasing the tablet.

Connor had almost nodded off when the voice from the overhead speaker jolted him awake. The woman in the blue vest behind the counter announced the arrival of flight 1262 from Memphis. Connor looked out the window at the 727 rolling to a stop at the gate. He watched as the ground crew attached the jetway to the plane, and shortly after that, the woman in the blue vest tapped the keypad next to the boarding door. The door opened with a buzz, and the awaiting passengers gathered their belongings in anticipation that they'd soon be leaving Tampa.

A few minutes after the gate door opened, a few passengers from the Memphis flight trickled into the terminal. As the flow of passengers picked up, Connor watched as they walked past, eager to get to wherever they were going. After the last passenger deplaned, the crew followed. Two flight attendants emerged from the jetway pulling suitcases behind them. No sign of Jessica.

Could she have traded flights?

Connor waited a few more minutes, but still no Jessica. He pulled his phone from his pocket to call Stephanie. His next play was to get Jessica's cell phone number and call her. He had a bad feeling that Boone was sitting in her apartment parking lot, or maybe the apartment itself, waiting for her.

When he looked up again, he saw Jessica step off the jetway. She passed the waiting passengers, who were already jostling for position in the heaving line, preparing to board the next flight out.

Connor had positioned himself behind a support column so Jessica wouldn't see him when she deplaned. Once she walked past, he stood up and followed her through the terminal.

He moved quickly, but not too quickly. When he caught up with her, he snatched the rolling suitcase out of her hand.

"Hello, again. We need to talk," he said. "It's about your daughter."

It took a moment for her to recognize him. "You?"

"A lot's happened since we talked at your apartment."

"I don't have anything else to say to you." She reached to yank the suitcase back, but she couldn't break Connor's grip.

"Keep your voice down," he said. "We're going to my car."

"The hell we are." She jerked on the suitcase again but found the same result.

"Your ex-husband is looking for the two of you. And he's found Stephanie."

She stopped. "What?"

Connor wanted to grab her wrist and urge her forward, but they were in public, and even though the airport was near empty, there were still eyeballs on them.

"Justin Friedman told me about the postcards." He kept his voice low. "How you asked him to write them out for you. No one is blackmailing you. You're sending them yourself so Freddie will think you're dead."

"I don't know what you're talking about."

"Cut the shit. Freddie sent someone down here to find you. Someone besides me. And he's already visited your daughter."

"Is she okay?"

"For now. Freddie's man went to her bakery, but she got away. She's at her rental property now. I'll take you there. He's still out there, though, and neither of you are going to be safe until I find out why he's here and what he wants. But first, I need you to tell me what happened twelve years ago."

Boone arrived at the Indian Rocks Beach public parking lot. He looked at his phone and traced the red line on the GPS map with his finger, following the route from the highway to the destination several hundred feet away. He stepped out of the car and walked down the sidewalk until he arrived at a small blue-and-white cottage. He checked the phone again to confirm it was the right place.

Moving around to the side of the house, he peered through the window to find Stephanie watching a small television propped on a stack of moving boxes. He walked around to the front door and directly into a short man carrying a white plastic bag. Startled, the delivery man jumped back and nearly dropped the sack on the sandy ground.

"You scared me," he said in broken English.

"Sorry about that," said Boone. "Must have sensed you were coming."

The deliveryman handed him the bag. Whatever was inside was hot. It smelled like Chinese dumplings.

"Did my wife pay for it already?"

The deliveryman nodded and walked away.

"Thank you."

Knocking on the door, he turned his back and stepped to the side, making sure the plastic bag and little else was visible through the peephole.

When the door opened, he turned around and pushed his way into the cottage, knocking Stephanie backward.

"Hi, Sydney." He handed her the bag. "Your father says hello."

"What do you want?"

"We're going to have a little chat later. But for now, just sit down and be quiet." He opened his suit jacket and flashed the holstered pistol. "Or I'll put a bullet in your head."

Boone locked the front door, pushed several moving

boxes in front of it to prevent a quick exit, then pulled the window shades down. When he returned to the kitchen, he sat on a small stool and placed his 9mm on the counter next to him. Then he took out his cell and dialed.

When Connor and Jessica arrived at his rental on the third floor of the parking garage, Connor tossed her suitcase into the trunk and walked toward the driver's door. An airport security vehicle idled with its headlights on in the adjacent aisle. Connor glanced at it and then back to Jessica. She saw it too. Had she made a run for it, he wouldn't be able to catch her. He wouldn't be able to protect her either.

"Go ahead and flag him down," said Connor. "But if you do, you and Stephanie will never be safe."

"How do I know I can trust you?"

"Your daughter trusts me. Plus, I'm all you got."

She stole another glance at the idling security vehicle and then opened the passenger door.

Connor fired the engine, eager to put the forty-minute drive to Stephanie's cottage behind them.

"So, here's how this works," said Connor. "I know you're Debra Blasko. I know you were married to Little Freddie, and I know you tried to fake your death to disappear with your daughter. What I don't know is whether he really thinks you're dead or not."

She let out a long sigh and dropped her head. "Of course he does. I was careful."

"But without bodies, how could you be confident he bought it?"

"What else was I supposed to do? I knew if I just ran off

he'd come looking for us, so I had to use what I had, which wasn't much. Fred was mixed up with some bad people. I didn't know how bad until I overheard one of his phone conversations. He was talking about a murder he committed in Cleveland. Then I started snooping around and found a second cell phone in the garage. I scrolled through the text messages, and it was clear Fred wasn't who I thought he was."

"Why didn't you go to the police?"

"If I'd gone to the police, I'd be dead. One of the text messages I read was from someone threatening him. Threatening the entire family. Whoever sent the message said they'd been watching him and knew about Sydney and me. They threatened to kill us both and bury us somewhere Fred would never find us. That's when I knew I had to get out of there. So, I decided to disappear and figured maybe Fred would think whoever sent that text message was behind it. That we actually were buried somewhere he'd never find us." She turned to Connor. "How did you figure it out?"

"When I talked to your daughter, I told her about the postcards, and I fed her the same line you gave me about someone blackmailing you. She was worried about you. I asked her if there was anyone she knew who could have gotten you wrapped up in this, and she told me about Justin Friedman."

"Shit."

"I tracked him down. It took me a while, but he remembered writing the postcards all those years ago. I got lucky because it seems his brain is pretty fried. A few more years under him, and he'll likely drink that memory away completely. Why did you send me to Steph—Sydney anyway? And risk blowing your cover?"

"Because she didn't know anything about it. I knew I had to give you something, and I figured since she didn't know anything, she wouldn't be of any help. I guess I was wrong. And fuck you for bringing this shit to Tampa."

"You brought this shit to Tampa the moment you decided to run. Not me. Fred hired me to find the person he thought killed you. That's it."

"So, he does think we're dead."

"I'm not sure anymore. He sent someone else down here with me. Someone who tailed me to Sydney's bakery, and God knows where else."

"Who is he?"

Connor pulled onto the airport terminal parkway. "He's the guy who does the stuff Fred used to do."

"Why is he here?"

"The way I see it, there are two options. Once Fred realized I was onto something, he sent his man down here to take out the person responsible for the murders."

"I thought that was your job."

"No. He hired me to find whoever was sending the postcards. I wasn't about to kill anyone for him."

"You said there were two options. What's the second one?"

"Fred doesn't think you're dead, and he sent his man down to either bring you back or—" Connor stopped.

"Or kill us?"

Connor checked his mirrors. "How did you change your identity? That takes some skill. Did you have help?"

"If you call the government help, then yes."

"You cut a deal? To turn over evidence on Freddie?"

"God, no. I wouldn't survive that. I found some information online about getting a new identity. Changing my name, getting a new driver's license and all that."

"None of that is easy," said Connor. "Trust me, I know. You'd need a new social security number to do any of that, and you can't just walk into the Social Security Administration and ask for a new one."

"You can if you're a battered wife."

Connor didn't answer.

"A friend of mine was in an abusive marriage. She was able to get a new social security number by proving her life was in danger. She had to provide police reports she filed against her husband and hospital records from the two times he put her in the ER. All that, along with a few testimonials from a cop and a nurse, and she got a new social. Changed her name and got the hell out of there. I called her, explained my situation and she told me exactly how to do it."

"But you didn't have those police reports or medical records."

"No, but I had a very sympathetic ear at the social security office, someone who had escaped a bad marriage and was willing to look the other way. With new numbers for Sydney and me, I became Jessica Winslow. She became Stephanie. We moved to Tampa, and here we are."

Debra looked over her shoulder as Connor pulled on the entrance ramp to I-275 South.

"Here's the thing that bothers me," he said. "Why now? If Little Freddie thought you might be alive, why wait twelve years to come looking for you? Seems he'd want to find you from the start."

"I don't know."

"Did you contact him or do anything else recently that might get him thinking you're still alive?"

"No," she said. "I haven't had any contact with him. Aside from the postcards."

"And there's no chance Sydney could have done something? Reached out to him?"

"Why would she do that?"

"I don't know, but something must have happened to get him looking for you after all this time."

"I told Sydney her father was dead and that he was a piece-of-shit criminal with friends who might come looking for us. I explained how we had to change our names and make a new life in Florida. Even at eleven, she understood that."

Connor squinted as an onslaught of headlights beamed through the windshield.

"So, what's your plan?" asked Debra.

"Once I know you two are together and safe, I'll get to the bottom of this."

Debra glanced over her shoulder again. "Why are you doing this?"

"You're in trouble, and I'm in the business of getting people out of trouble."

Connor was about thirty miles from Indian Rocks Beach when his phone rang. It was on the third ring when Connor realized it wasn't his personal cell, but the one Little Freddie had given him.

"Connor?" said the man on the other end of the line.

He recognized the voice.

"I'm at the beach house, and I've got your baker. I don't want her, though, only Debra. Bring her to the beach house, and you and Sydney can walk away."

"I don't know where she is," said Connor.

"Bullshit. The girl says you went to the airport to get her. You've got an hour. Bring Debra here, or I kill this one. Slowly." The line went dead.

"They've got Sydney?" Debra smacked the phone out of his hand. "You said she was safe."

Connor realized his miscalculation as the phone bounced off the console and fell to his feet. Little Freddie hadn't given him the phone for updates. He'd been tracking him.

That's how he found the bakery and the beach house.

"We need to go to the police," said Debra.

"That's a bad idea."

"But Sydney—"

"I'll get her."

"How? What are you going to do?"

"I have experience fixing things when they go sideways. I'll get your daughter."

Connor exited the highway, doubled back a few miles, and stopped at a stoplight next to a convertible. He reached for Little Freddie's cell phone on the floor and flicked it into the back seat of the convertible as the light turned green. A few minutes later, they arrived at Debra's apartment.

"Do you have a weapon in there?"

"No. I hate guns."

"Me too, but sometimes they come in handy." He handed

her his personal cell phone. "Put your number in there, and I'll call when this is over."

"If my daughter's there, I'm coming with you."

"No way in hell. You're staying right here until this is over."

"I heard him say he'd kill her if I didn't come."

"He came to Tampa to kill you and likely me too. You show up at that beach house, and you're dead. He'll kill you regardless."

"I can't just sit up there and wait for a telephone call."

"Look, we don't have a lot of time, and the longer we spend arguing, the less time I have to get over there."

Debra closed her eyes tight, thought for a moment, then typed her number into Connor's cell phone. She handed the phone to Connor, unlocked the passenger door and stepped out.

"Get her back," she said.

"I'll get her."

He kicked the rental into gear and tore out of the parking lot.

19

PLAN B

BOONE WATCHED Sydney as she stared at the plastic bag in front of her.

"You should eat," he said. "It may be a while before you get another chance."

"I don't really have an appetite."

He clicked on his cell phone and studied the screen. "Looks like they're making a run for it."

"What?"

"Connor. He's going in the wrong direction."

"Good," she said. "I hope he gets my mother far away from here."

When Connor arrived at the beach public parking lot, he already had a plan in his head. The small footprint of the cottage was a problem. With a larger home he could enter through the basement or the second floor, but with only three rooms, Sydney's place didn't present many options. In the Army, he'd participated in too many close-quarter combat trainings to count, and that training provided a significant advantage.

There were five elements required for a successful assault. Detailed planning, surprise, method of entry, violence of action, and speed. He knew Sydney's vacation home because he'd been there. It was only for a few minutes, but it gave him enough time to note the layout, the choke points, and the obstacles he'd need to avoid. The element of surprise was on his side, he hoped. Boone would have realized by now the cell phone was traveling away from the beach house. Whether or not he bought it was another matter. Connor also knew how he'd enter the property, but that was more a point of availability, not strategy. The front door was out, as were the windows in the living room. His only option was the bedroom window. It was the only entry point not visible from the main room.

The last two elements, violence of action and speed, were up in the air. There's a reason SWAT teams repel down ropes and smash through windows even though they don't have to. That violent action creates a psychological advantage, stirs up a shit-ton of confusion, and puts the enemy on their heels. Connor didn't have that in his toolbox. Speed was likely also out. Connor would have to enter quietly, and the house was too small to generate a lot of momentum, though he'd conjure up what he could.

Connor studied the area before he stepped out of the car. There was a beach party with two dozen people drinking and dancing around a twenty-foot bonfire a hundred feet away from the lot. A few couples walked the beach, while a handful of others watched the calm surf ebb and flow. It was too dark to see anything else.

He popped the trunk, walked behind the car, and removed the carpeted trunk liner. An unimpressive car jack and tire iron were latched to the bottom with plastic fasteners. He popped the tire iron out and jostled it in his hand. It was light for a piece of metal, but it would have to do. He preferred a straight iron. Those were easier to swing. This one looked like a metal plus sign with four different sized lug nut wrenches on the ends. Not ideal.

The plank boardwalk that led from the parking lot to the beach houses was out. Boone would be eyeballing that from the house, and Connor wasn't about to give him advance notice of his arrival. There was one thing the boardwalk had going for it, though. The palm trees that flanked the boardwalk offered a place to stash the tire iron in case Connor needed it later. This model was too large and would be clumsy in a close-quarter fight. There was also a chance Connor could drop it during a scuffle and find it buried in his own skull. Given a choice, he preferred using his fists. They were more versatile than this hunk of metal and, when used correctly, just as dangerous. That didn't mean the tire iron was useless. It just wasn't Plan A.

Connor looked over his shoulder and checked the bonfire crowd, who seemed to have no idea he was there. He crouched and placed the tire iron at the base of the third palm tree from the parking lot, nearly slicing his hand open on the tree's sharp bark. After tilting it just right and pressing it into the sand, it was concealed from anyone not looking for it. He didn't think he'd see it again. It was only there if things went south.

Connor dashed off the boardwalk and strolled a quarter-mile out of his way so he could approach Sydney's home directly from the rear, the only side with no windows. The clouds blowing in from the sea swallowed up any moonlight, allowing Connor to approach in near darkness.

When he arrived at the home, he made his way to the bedroom window. Peering inside, he could see Sydney sitting alone in the living room. Boone wasn't in sight, but Connor knew he was in there somewhere. Likely near the front door so he could cut off Sydney's exit and Connor's entry. The bedroom was the only blind spot.

The solitary bedroom window was the horizontal type that slid open to the side. This style usually had two latches, one at the top and one at the bottom, but this one was a cheaper model. It only had one latch in the center. Lucky break.

There are two ways to open this type of window from the outside. One method requires inserting a thin piece of wire between the panes. Simply loop it around the latch and pull it open. He had no wire. That left option two. Horizontal windows ran on tracks, and by applying the right amount of pressure, they could be easily popped off.

After checking that no one was watching, Connor removed the screen from the window and placed his hands on the glass. He pushed in on the window and to the right, toward the latch. By carefully rocking the window back and forth, he could lift it off the track, pulling it away from the latch. When done quickly, the maneuver was effective but loud. Since there was an armed man inside the house, loud wasn't an option. Connor had to take it slow. He gently pushed on the window, applying as much force as he could without shattering it. He pushed to the right and up, trying to dislodge the pane from the locking mechanism. After a minute, he had rocked the window enough that it was pulling away from the track. A few more tries, and it popped off the latch. Connor carefully lifted the window out of the frame and set it inside on the floor. After checking over his shoulder again, he climbed into the bedroom.

Boone sat in the kitchen watching Sydney consider the now cold Styrofoam container. He thought about calling Connor's cell phone again, but he assumed he'd already tossed it. Connor may not have realized he was being tracked from the beginning, but he'd know now. It was the only explanation for him discovering the beach house. That wouldn't escape Connor.

He thought he heard something from the side of the house. A slight popping sound. The noise itself wasn't enough to warrant attention, but the sound combined with the sudden change in pressure and the burst of humid, salty air wasn't something he planned to ignore.

Inside the bedroom, the scent of Chinese food hit Connor. Something spicy. He crept to the door, which was open half-way, and peered through the narrow gap between the door hinges and the wall. Sydney sat with her head down, staring into her food, but he couldn't see anyone else. He shallowed his breath, convinced it was loud enough to hear throughout the house. When he looked at Sydney again, she wasn't looking down at her food. She was looking right at him.

Boone would see her looking too. Time to move.

Connor exploded into the room and charged right into

the big man, who was coming to check the bedroom. Connor threw two heavy right hands just below his left eye. Both connected, but he didn't go down. Connor surged forward, looking to snap Boone's kneecap with his boot, but he was quick for his size. Boone pivoted out of the way and Connor's foot landed awkwardly on the side of a paint can. As Connor struggled for balance, Boone lunged, taking them both to the ground.

Two quick punches found Connor's ribs before Boone climbed on top of him. He wrapped his right arm around Connor's neck and tightened his grip in a rear choke. Knowing he was seconds away from blacking out, Connor tilted his chin and found the gap in the V of Boone's elbow. It bought him a few more seconds of consciousness, and he used it to his advantage. Next to them were two unopened paint cans, an aluminum paint tray, and a hammer. He reached out and found the hammer as Boone repositioned his arm and reapplied the choke. This time he locked it in, and Connor felt his trachea collapsing. He swung the hammer wildly behind him. The first two swings missed, but the third connected with something. Air rushed back into Connor's lungs, and he struggled to his feet. As he found his balance, a fist the size of a beer can slammed into his lower jaw. The room went dark before Connor hit the ground.

When Connor opened his eyes, he was sitting on the kitchen floor with his back against the refrigerator. The left side of his face was numb. His vision was blurry, but slowly returned as he blinked the fog away.

Boone stood over him. Sydney was sitting on the floor

near the bedroom door, her legs pulled toward her body. Her face was buried in her knees, and she rocked back and forth like a kid trying to block something out. Shock was setting in.

"Where's Debra?" asked Boone.

Connor tried to rub his jaw, but his arms were taped behind him. He looked down to find his legs taped at the knees and ankles.

"Where is she?" he repeated.

"Not here." Connor was surprised his jaw still worked. "She's long gone."

Boone picked up the 9mm from the counter and raised it to Connor's face. "I don't ask twice."

Connor's brain wasn't firing as clearly as it was before hitting Boone's fist with his face, but he knew Little Freddie's man wasn't going to shoot him. He was all threat and no leverage.

"I think Little Freddie would be a bit pissed if you killed the only person who knows where his wife is."

Boone drove his black wingtip into Connor's knee. The blinding pain hit him before the cracking sound. When the pain subsided enough for him to see again, he looked up.

"Beat me all you want. I'm not telling you anything."

"You'll talk."

"No, I won't," said Connor. "You're dealing with an ex-Army interrogator. I'm not going to tell you anything, even if I die right here on this floor."

Boone thought for a moment, went into the living room, and returned with Sydney. He kicked her legs out from under her, pressed her face against the kitchen countertop, and placed the 9mm to the back of her head.

"Last chance. Where's Debra?"

Connor shook his head. "You're big, and you have a hellava left hook." He tasted blood in his mouth. "But you're not going to kill her either."

"That so?"

"I figure you were sent here to kill Debra, but not her. Little Freddie won't take kindly to you offing Sydney." Yes, definitely blood. "We both know you're not going to kill Freddie's only daughter. You've got no leverage."

Boone thought through his options. Connor needed him to realize where Debra was, or at least where Debra might be, and then drag Connor and Sydney there with him. If Connor was to survive this, he needed to get out of the beach house. And he wasn't going to get out on his own.

Boone pushed Sydney to the ground and then grabbed his cell phone and tapped the screen. When he looked back at Connor, his eyes were brighter than a moment ago. "You took her back to her apartment. That's the first place I went when I got to Florida."

"Why would I do that?"

"Because it's safe there. You're not going to the police. You wouldn't bring her here. Too dangerous. You'd stash her somewhere. Her apartment likely. That way, she can pack her bags and be ready in case you have to run for it."

Boone was connecting the dots Connor hoped he'd connect, and now it was time to go. He had to take Connor and Sydney with him. He couldn't risk leaving them here alone, and besides, if Debra wasn't at her apartment, he'd have to go back to the drawing board with Connor.

"Get up," he said, grabbing Sydney by the arm and

pushing her against the front door. "Put your hands in your pockets."

She did, and he grabbed the duct tape and wrapped a thick strip around her waist, trapping her hands inside her pockets. He pushed her aside and then looped his arm through Connor's arms and lifted him to his feet. "You next." He jerked the tape from Connor's hands, nearly dislocating his wrists.

Connor complied, and Boone wrapped a thick strip around Connor's waist. He tore the tape from the roll and then added a second wrap.

Conor expected to talk himself out of the beach house, but he hadn't counted on the tape. It was a smart move. In the darkness, it would look like Connor and Sydney were simply walking with their hands in their pockets. Much more natural than having their hands tied behind their backs.

Boone ripped the two tape bands from Connor's legs and then pushed them both out the front door. He followed close behind, gripping the silenced 9mm inside his suit jacket.

"Walk."

Connor led the way to the boardwalk. He assumed Boone had parked there because there were few other options. He walked at Sydney's pace, staying close to her side. The bonfire crew still partied on the beach. After a few minutes on the boardwalk, the public parking lot came into view. Conor knew what would happen next, and it wasn't good. Boone would toss Connor and Sydney into the trunk, or maybe the back seat, and then drive to Debra's apartment. He was right to check there. If he knew which apartment she was in, she wouldn't last long. He'd kick the door down and plug her. Then he'd come back for Connor. Game over.

Connor fixed his eyes on the palm trees ahead. Sydney slowed, and Boone nudged her forward with a massive shoulder. Connor's eyes shifted between the palm trees and Sydney's feet. When they were close enough, he stepped in front of her. Her left foot tripped over his right and she stumbled forward, taking two quick steps before losing her balance and tumbling off the right side of the boardwalk. Connor slipped off the left. When Boone reached for Sydney, Connor was already twisting his lower back against the sharp palm tree bark, shredding the duct tape and part of his shirt. Sydney was nearly to her feet when Connor found the tire iron. Connor swept Sydney's legs, dropping her again. He wanted her out of the way. When Boone turned, the tire iron connected with his jaw. Teeth and bone fragments littered the boardwalk.

Plan B.

Big Boone went down but braced his fall with his hands. As he tried to stand, Connor swung again, connecting to the side of his head. Boone twitched violently. Connor brought the tire iron down again. The twitching stopped. It was over in seconds.

Connor helped Sydney to her feet, ripped the duct tape from her waist, and they ran the rest of the way to Connor's rental. The bonfire seemed to be dying down, and Connor wondered how long it would take someone to find the dead man on the boardwalk.

"Are you okay?" he asked.

She nodded but didn't raise her head.

"It's okay. It's over."

"Where's my mother?" she asked through her hands.

"She's safe. Back at her place." He pulled her hands

down and wiped her face with his sleeve. She was shaking. He wrapped his arms around her and pulled her close. "You're safe. Everything is going to be okay."

Sydney looked toward the boardwalk. "Is he dead?"

"With a hole that deep in his head, he's better off."

20

LOOSE ENDS

CONNOR ARRIVED in Cincinnati the following day. It had been a long drive.

It only took a few phone calls to track down Little Freddie's address. He was easier to locate than his wife and daughter had been.

Little Freddie lived in a small town north of the city. The kind of town that got quiet when the sun went down. The kind of town with small homes on small lots close to one another.

The Craftsman style home on Orchard Avenue had forest-green cedar siding with cream-colored trim and flower boxes outside the second-story windows. The home looked like something you'd find on the Hallmark Channel, not housing a contract killer.

Connor found the back door locked, but that wasn't much of a deterrent. Locks are like people. Push hard enough, and they'll break. He stepped back, drew in a deep breath, and surged forward, sending his two-hundred-ten-pound frame into the door. It snapped open without much of a fight. Once inside, he moved fast, bounding through the kitchen and into the living room, where he found Little Freddie sitting on the sofa.

Little Freddie started to get up but stopped when he saw the silenced 9mm in Connor's hand. It looked familiar. Like the one his enforcer carried.

"Boone's dead," said Connor.

"I figured as much." He leaned forward on the sofa. "And my wife and daughter?" Little Freddie sat up straight and readjusted his robe.

"Safe," said Connor. "When did you realize there were alive? Did you always know?"

"No. Debra had a good thing going. I bought it until I got the most recent postcard."

"What changed your mind?"

"Tiptoes. Sydney's nickname. No one but Debra and I would know that." He leaned back and sunk into the sofa. "I didn't want to believe it. I'd spent so long hating someone for taking them away from me. Then to find out it was Debra all along." He shook his head. "But that hate, it had to go somewhere. I'm surprised you found her."

"So, you used me," said Connor.

"I didn't use you."

"You kept me in the dark."

"You wouldn't have helped me if you knew the whole story."

"You're right about that."

"Tell me about them," said Little Freddie.

"Debra is working for an airline. Has been since she moved to Tampa."

"A flight attendant? That's funny. She never had the disposition for that. What about Sydney?"

"She runs a bakery. I hear it's pretty good."

"Is she happy?"

"I suspect she was until all this shit happened."

Little Freddie's muscles tensed as if he was about to use them.

"What was your endgame?" asked Connor. "You plan to kill them both?"

"Just Debra."

"Why?"

"Because I'm a bitter old man, and she robbed me of twelve years with my only daughter." He eyeballed the weapon in Connor's hand. "What's your endgame? You come here to kill me?"

"Reckon I have no other choice."

"Why's that?"

"You're a loose end. If I don't kill you, you'll come after me, and I have enough enemies. With me out of the way, you'd go after Debra and Sydney again. I suspect you'd eventually find them. I can't have that either."

"That is a pickle, isn't it?" Little Freddie was calm, as if he'd been in this situation before. "I've got powerful friends. Even if you kill me, they'll come for you. I've taken precautions."

"I suspect you have."

There was no weapon on the coffee table, but Little Freddie was the type of person who'd have one stashed nearby.

"Maybe we could come up with another arrangement," said Little Freddie. "One that suits us both."

"No time," said Connor. "I've got to return this rental car and catch a flight. Heading back to Maine to finish my vacation."

"That's unfortunate."

It was the last thing Little Freddie said before Connor pulled the trigger.

21

MR. FISH

CONNOR SAT at the bar at Palmer's. He was three bites into a chicken salad sandwich when the front door chimed. Foot-steps followed. It wasn't the heavy boot stomps that were typical there. It was a long shot, but he hoped it was Tara. He didn't like the way they left things, and while he planned to visit her in North Carolina, life had a habit of getting in the way. He looked up from his lunch and peered into the mirror behind the bar, hoping he'd recognize the reflection of a brunette in high heels. Nothing.

As he chomped away, the telephone behind the bar rang. For a moment, Connor considered grabbing it off the cradle, but then he remembered what his father used to say. *Never answer another man's phone without permission.*

He let it ring, and eventually, Palmer stepped out of the kitchen and answered with his familiar Down East accent. If you listened long enough, you'd swear it was Jimmy Stewart.

"Ya, he's here then." Palmer stretched the cord across the bar and handed the receiver to Connor. "It's fer you."

"Hello?"

"You're a hard man to track down. Been calling your cell for two hours. Then I remembered I had this number."

The man on the other end of the line was Mr. Fish, Connor's friend and business partner in Boston.

"No cell service on the island," said Connor. "Came to the mainland for lunch. What's going on?"

"I have a new client, Denise Rodriquez. Just talked to her this morning. Need to help her and her daughter disappear. Seems her husband"—paper rustled on the other end—"Ernesto is a shot caller for some Boston gang. She wants out, and he won't let her."

"She worth the effort?" asked Connor.

"I think so."

"Timeline?"

"I'm working on the documents now," said Mr. Fish. "I'll have new identities for the two of them in a week or so. I could use your help with the extraction."

Connor thought back to Debra's story about getting her new identity by going straight to the Social Security Administration and citing spousal abuse. That approach didn't work for people like Denise Rodriquez, even if she did check all the boxes. That's why Mr. Fish was in high demand. He was an equal-opportunity resource, and he'd made more people disappear than David Copperfield.

"A week?" said Connor. "I'm in."

"When are you getting back from Maine?"

"Leaving tomorrow." He looked in the mirror again. "But I don't think I'm coming straight home. Making a pit stop in North Carolina."

"For how long?"

"That depends on someone else, but I'll be back before you need me."

"Good enough."

The line went dead. Conor wrestled the tangled cord from around his elbow and handed it back to Palmer.

"All gravy?" asked Palmer.

"Never better."

Connor stuffed the last chunk of chicken salad into his mouth, paid the tab and tip, and walked to the boat Mitch Skinner had loaned him. The lake was calm, and from the dock, Connor could see the bottom as clearly as if he were looking through a window. He started the boat, untied the lines, and steered toward his family's island, knowing it would be some time before he saw Palmer's again. He was itching to pack up and leave in the morning, maybe more keen than he had ever been to leave Maine.

He was eager to see what awaited him in North Carolina.

CONNOR HARDING WILL RETURN

Continue the Connor Harding series with:

MIRAGE MAN

AUTHOR'S NOTE

SIGN UP FOR MY E-NEWSLETTER for updates and free fiction.

If you want to stay on top of my new releases, get free fiction, or snag exclusive deals, sign up for my author newsletter at www.traceconger.com/freebies.

CONSIDER LEAVING A REVIEW

Like this book? Consider leaving a review at your favorite online bookstore. Reviews from readers like you can help other readers find their next favorite read. And it's a great way to support your favorite authors.

Thanks for the eyeballs.

Trace Conger

Cincinnati, Ohio

ACKNOWLEDGMENTS

If I knew that writing would be this tough, I'd have given it up long ago. Luckily, there's a team of people behind me who push me onward. I want to thank the following people for their direct and indirect involvement in jolting this book to life.

Andrew Bockhold for reading early drafts and providing thoughtful advice that literally changed the course of this novel. Jeff Hillard for being a friend, sounding board, and guide along this absurd journey. Elizabeth White for polishing this bad boy up like a sweet chrome fender. The Miami Valley Writers Network, especially April Wilson, for sharing your insight and knowledge.

Thank you also to D.M. and B.L. for spilling trade secrets and to Jessica Drossart, Bill Swisher, and Lisa Garrell for providing me a backstage pass into their worlds.

And finally, thank you to my amazing family, who encourage and inspire me every day.

ABOUT THE AUTHOR

Trace Conger is an award-winning author in the crime, thriller, and suspense genres. He writes the Connor Harding (Thriller) series and the Mr. Finn (PI) series, among others.

His Connor Harding series follows freelance "Mirage Man" Connor Harding as he solves problems for the world's most dangerous criminals. The Mr. Finn series follows private investigator Finn Harding as he straddles the fine line between right and wrong.

Conger won a Shamus Award for his debut novel, THE SHADOW BROKER. His suspense novella, THE WHITE BOY, won the Fresh Ink Award for Best Novella of 2020.

He is known for his tight writing style, dark themes, and subtle humor. Trace lives in Cincinnati with his wonderfully supportive family.

ALSO BY TRACE CONGER